Memento mori. Latin.

(Rough translation: "Remember that you must die.")

Memento Mortale. Latin elements.

(Rough translation: "Remember the Mortale family.")

ALSO BY ANGELINE WALSH

The Reign of Victoria; or, the Year That Everything Changed

Bad Psychiatry and Other Aptly Themed Poems

CHAPTER ONE

IT WAS ON May the thirteenth that events took a turn for the Mortale family. They had been going about their usual Saturday morning business. Mildred, the youngest child—fourteen years of age come autumn—had already experienced a personally unpleasant morning. She had been standing over Mortem's grave, having just finished inscribing a humble homemade headstone, when the telephone rang with the news. She was summoned inside immediately, without even having the chance to place flowers over the delicate patch of newly disturbed soil. After a few solemn, meditative moments to take in the somber news, the Mortale family hailed a carriage to their destination.

THE SICKROOM WAS draped in the thickness of grief. Mildred stood silently beside her mother as Aunt Ola wailed on and on about the tremendous tragedy, how her beautiful Lucia had been untroubled the moment she had passed, having found peace at last after a few long, tumultuous days of the sinister sickness that had swept across the city that summer, what the people were calling "the devil's disease." All the while, Mildred's eyes drifted toward the bed.

Lucia hadn't been the kindest of cousins. Mildred and Lucia were hardly what one would call close, but to see Lucia like this—stiff and pale grey like a statue—awakened pity in Mildred. As Aunt Ola made her rounds, smothering everyone in tear-stained hugs and muffled sniffs, Mildred memorized the image of her cousin. Despite how snubbing, impetuous, rude, and snobbish she had been, Lucia hadn't been able to finagle her way out of it—the sickness had defeated her in the end, and Aunt Ola and Uncle Edmund's large fortune hadn't been able to do a thing to prevent it.

THE RIDE BACK home was just as quiet and stifling as the trip preceding. Mildred, her hands neatly folded on her lap, observed the passing scenery with a breath of newfound gratitude for her life. Her sister, Morgan, had been the only one in the family to cry during the visit. She'd been the one closest to Lucia amongst the Mortale siblings—most likely because of their shared ego and snippiness. Morgan delicately dabbed a glistening eye with a white lace-edged handkerchief.

When, at last, the carriage pulled up alongside the curb in front of the Mortale home, the family shuffled out and silently made their way inside. Coats and hats were hung on the coat rack by the door, gloves were slipped off, and sighs were released. Everyone went about their separate ways, bound for yet another dull and senseless day indoors.

Since the advent of the yellow fever, Mother prohibited anyone in the household from stepping outside for longer than the measure of a few heartbeats, for the adamant fear of the disease in the air being absorbed into any of her children's fragile bodies. (They were allowed allotted time to sit in the garden in the backyard, but that mostly consisted of squirrel-watching with the occasional game of spider-racing, a game Mildred's brother Marley had invented.)

So, the Mortale residence remained unnervingly silent for the remainder of the afternoon, except for the one extremely loud hour that Mother spent on the telephone, jabbering to all and any acquaintance she could about the great family tragedy. The telephone was something that Father had resisted installing; he railed against anything "modern", not for political or religious reasons, but because the growing popularity of electric lights and technology in homes had rendered his kerosene lamp and candle company increasingly obsolete.

"I know, it's the most horrible thing," Mother sighed into the speaker. "None of us would have ever anticipated the disease to infect *our* family..." She twisted the telephone's cord around a finger as she tilted her head and looked pleasantly bored with her friend's response.

Mildred, who sat perched on the bottom step of the staircase, balancing her chin on her fist, managed to nearly escape her mother's obnoxious prattling, her eyes slowly and sleepily fluttering closed—but they just as soon popped open again when she heard her name uttered.

"Oh, yes, Mildred is going to be alright," Mother said, with great indifference. "Just the same as always, you know..."

Whatever Mother meant to clarify about this statement, Mildred would never know, because, at that instant, a tremendous BOOM emanated from the basement. Mother, startled by the sudden noise (or perhaps, as Mildred suspected, merely surprised that something could possibly be louder than she was), jumped with a shriek, still clutching the telephone cord, causing an even more terrible shock for her when the phone was ripped directly from the wall by the force of her recoil. As she gasped in disbelief at the gaping hole in the wall, the telephone fixture dangling pathetically from the wallpaper, the basement door flung open, and out popped Marley, sooty and sputtering.

"What did you do?" Mother screeched, her face glowing a nice shade of pink.

Marley shrugged, tugging off a pair of gloves with quick precision. Before any more interrogations could occur, he stole up the stairs, sending a cloud of dark, fine dust (or, at least, what she suspected to be dust) into Mildred's face as he passed her.

"I can't believe it," Mother mumbled exasperatedly as she stared in horror at the limp telephone cord coiled around her fingers. Mildred smiled to herself, safely out of the range of Mother's sight.

DINNER THAT EVENING was extraordinarily uncomfortable. Marley didn't speak a word, hardly even glancing up from his plate, on which he absentmindedly scraped around bits of food with his fork. It had taken him hours to scrub away the mysterious post-explosive debris and even still, smudges were visible here and there. No one had dared ask him what had happened and, of course, none of them could enter the basement to see for themselves. The basement had been Marley's workspace and domain for years and was kept secure with a myriad of strategically placed locks and chains.

Mother sat stiff-backed with pursed lips, grieving over the death of the telephone.

Morgan was her usual silently reserved self.

Mildred attempted to lighten up the mood by smiling warmly in Father's direction. His melancholy mood persisted. In Mildred's experience, his silence was far worse than anything else, even rage. Father's silence meant that he was deeply submerged in a pensive, solemn state, one that, unlike anger, failed to subside quickly. Moods like this went on for days, and sometimes weeks. When he was like this, Father wouldn't have cared if Marley had blown the house to bits of rubble.

The distasteful atmosphere was elevated by yet another sample of Mother's so-called "experimental cooking." Mildred poked at her dinner, barely taking a bite of what she could hardly identify as food. Since Father's business had taken a toll for the worse, they'd had to let go of their longtime household staff, which had, unfortunately, included the cook, a matronly woman respected by the family for both her wonderful tact and excellent Sunday roast.

It had been a rough start to the spring. Not long after Father drudgingly announced to the family that his store had declared bankruptcy, the home had swiftly become stripped of familiar things. Mildred had watched from the upstairs foyer while strange men marched in and out of the house, taking with them cabinets and armoires, sculptures and oil paintings, drawers of silverware, and sets of china teacups. They unscrewed the chandelier from the foyer ceiling and emptied the guest bedroom until all that was left was a floor, walls, and a lonely window. Mother sniffled as she packed away mounds of clothing and party dresses and jewelry for auction. The servants left soon after—all three housemaids, the butler, and the cook. They looked so dismal, shuffling out the door all in a row, like a pitiful parade, waving their goodbyes in dejected silence.

"All of our old money, gone," Mother had cried. Mildred didn't ask what she meant.

It had been a long time coming, admittedly. Even before the great purging, the home had seemed to Mildred like a neglected museum, full of fine old things that no one properly cared for. Now, the rooms were too full of echoes, and she could feel the emptiness as if it were a physical thing. Mother had insisted on keeping a few of the old paintings, which still dotted the house. And there was the family photograph that had been taken in the previous spring, which hung above the fireplace in the drawing room. The five people in the portrait appeared reserved and self-assured, none having a suspicion of what would happen over the course of a year.

Father cleared his throat and spoke his first words of the day. "What happened to that old cat...uh, what was his name again? ...Oh, never mind. Anyway, I haven't seen him around much lately."

Mildred looked up and said, sorrowfully, "He's—"

"Dead," blurted Marley.

Father's brows knit with concern. "When and how did this happen?"

"This morning," Mildred sighed, rolling around some shriveled peas on her plate. "Well, at least that's when I found him. I haven't the slightest idea of what happened. I buried him out in the front garden this morning, just before we left.

Mother's head perked up, her eyes wide in horror. "The garden? Why would you do such a thing? Please tell me you didn't upset the tulips!"

"It's nicer than the backyard garden," Mildred remarked.

"That's a shame," Father said, ignoring any concerns about gardens and shaking his head slowly. "He was a good cat."

"Yes. And only still a baby, practically," Mildred added. "One year old, in June."

"That's not much of a baby age in cat years," Marley mumbled.

"Oh, you shut up!" Mildred spat. Marley winced as a pea flew off her fork and into his direction.

"Mortem was a fine pet, and he will not be forgotten." Mother closed the dispute rather sternly, giving both Mildred and Marley wary glances.

"Well," sighed Father, standing from his place, his dinner untouched, "I'll be back to my work now. If anyone needs me, I'll be in the study, as always."

With these as his final words, he turned at once and went directly down the hall. Father spent most of his time in the study when he was in his quiet mood, poring over books and documents. He had once wanted to study to become a doctor but instead inherited the family business. Now, in the advent of the fever, he wished he'd become a doctor, after all.

After the table had been cleared, Mildred escaped the tension and headed outdoors. Mother called after her to inquire where she was going, but Mildred simply ignored the questions and ran out the front door, letting it creak shut behind her and proceeding directly to Mortem's gravesite. However, the moment she reached her pet's resting place, a cold feeling charged through her—dirt was strewn everywhere, leaving an ugly hole in the garden. Mother would be horrified.

Worst of all, the grey stone marker she'd so lovingly made had been tossed into a bed of daisies (thank goodness they weren't the tulips). Beside herself in confusion, Mildred knelt at the newly unearthed burial site and tried to steady her breathing. After just a few moments, however, her befuddlement was very quickly replaced with a raging realization.

"*Where is he?*" Mildred bellowed as she rushed inside, marching pointedly toward Marley, who was seated studiously at the drawing room desk, furiously scribbling away into a tattered notebook opened to a page filled with various complicated diagrams and sketches.

"Are you referring to Mortem, perhaps?"

"I am," Mildred replied, her hands on her hips.

Marley paused his pen and glanced upwards. "Do you wish to see him?"

Mildred's stomach lurched suddenly, a reel of gruesome images flashing in her mind. "What have you done to him?"

"Nothing much, yet." Marley shrugged.

"What are you *planning* on doing to him?" Mildred's pulse quickened as she tried to suppress various ideas as to what might become of the carcass in Marley's eagerly gloved hands.

Ever since he was a small child, Marley had a fascination with dead things which, when he'd grown older, had developed into a dissection habit. Mother had been appalled and disgusted by this behavior but Father, who possessed a certain passion for the medical and anatomical himself, encouraged Marley's hobbies in hopes of him pursuing a future medical career. Mildred had grown to think that she was the only one who knew for certain that Marley's intentions weren't purely educational.

"Do you not wish to know the cause of his death?" Marley inquired.

Mildred considered, with hesitant curiosity, Mortem's tragic ending. But the thought of her much-loved pet being sliced open and who knows what else was stronger still. She stood a little taller, lifted her chin, and crossed her arms in defiant confidence. "No."

"No?" Marley sighed. "Hm. Alright, then." He then grumbled to himself, "What am I going to do with him now?"

"Leave him alone in peace, like he was before you so rudely interrupted!" quipped Mildred, turning straight for the basement door, enraged enough to beat down the door herself, chains and all.

Marley jumped up from his chair and reached the door just before Mildred did. "I'll get him. Just wait here a minute."

"Fine," Mildred sighed. "But be quick about it."

Straightaway (after rapidly unlocking the locks with a key he procured from his pocket) Marley bolted down the basement steps. There was a bit of rummaging clatter from below, which concerned Mildred somewhat, but just about a minute later Marley reappeared at the top of the steps with a white cloth-covered, cat-shaped lump in his arms.

"Alright," he said, quite out of breath, kicking the door shut behind him. "How about we have a proper burial?"

"Really?" Mildred's spirits lifted a bit; it had been a while since Marley had voluntarily done a nice thing for her. Although this struck her as somewhat suspicious, she accepted the offer with gratitude.

They went outdoors. Marley placed the body carefully into the crevice in the soil, and both stood with hands folded neatly before them. Marley cleared his throat and started his speech while Mildred gently sprinkled catnip over the sheeted figure.

"Mortem was a beloved feline. He was born on..."

"June the eighth."

"...June the eighth, and was especially adored by Mildred Mortale, who made sure he always had his favorite toys and foods, and who always kept his coat perfectly shiny and parasite-free. She spoiled him and overfed him, but we'll overlook those facts in this sad moment. He met an unfortunate early fate on May the twelfth—or perhaps it was the thirteenth, we don't know for certain—hardly a year old. All the members of the family will miss him dearly."

"I just want to have one last look at him, you know, before I say goodbye," Mildred said. She bent down and her fingers had hardly braised the white cloth when they were slapped away.

"What are you doing?" she gasped.

Marley averted Mildred's disdainful stare. "You don't want to remember him this way, Mildred. It'll give you nightmares, I'm sure of it."

Mildred avoided Marley's recommendation and, as quickly as she could, lifted away the cloth. It wasn't Mortem who lie under the sheets, after all; it was another cat entirely, this one white and grey, and in a quite gruesome state.

"Marley!" Mildred shrieked, hardly able to contain her disgust. She lowered her voice. "Is this Mrs. Pepperman's missing cat?"

Mrs. Pepperman was the well-meaning but vastly unstable elderly lady who lived next door. Her husband had died ages ago, and no one knew a thing about him, except that he was, according to the local gossip, murdered by Mrs. Pepperman. The lady's only constant in her life was her cat, Salty, who was just as old and deranged as Mrs. Pepperman herself. Salty had gone missing nearly a month ago. Mrs. Pepperman hadn't been seen since.

"Uh, yes," Marley answered after a bit.

"How could you?"

"Salty practically came to *me*," Marley said.

"Yes, of course." Mildred shook her head in disbelief.

"No, she did, I can assure you," Marley objected. "I was sitting just here, on the front porch, one afternoon, sketching, and she came over to me."

"What did you do to her, then?" Mildred inferred.

"Nothing, honestly," Marley continued. "She just came over, gave a soft meow, and then—just like that—she dropped dead at my feet. I didn't want to break Mrs. Pepperman's poor, fragile heart, so I just took Salty downstairs and ran a few tests on her. I didn't even have to harm her one bit."

Although sneaky and suspicious, Mildred had never known Marley to lie outright. She nodded slowly, trying to accept this bizarre tale. "So, I guess I don't want to know what you've already done to Mortem."

"It'd best not to know," Marley replied, and, with a lingering glance at the sorry grave, walked away.

IT WAS ABOUT six o'clock when the doorbell rang, followed by a set of impatient knocks. Mother rushed to the door as quickly as she could. Mildred, who sat in her usual place at the bottom of the staircase, was in the ideal spot to see this mysterious late evening visitor, who, once the door had been swung open, turned out to be Aunt Ola, looking gloomy as ever.

"Hello, Maria." Aunt Ola greeted Mother with a nod, wrapping her shawl closer to her body to shield herself from the vengeful wind that the impending storm had whipped up outside.

"Please, step inside," Mother insisted, opening the door a bit wider. "The air is giving me chills just standing here."

Aunt Ola gave a weak smile and stepped into the foyer. Mother gently closed the heavy front door, blocking out the vicious wind.

"Would you like to sit down?" Mother asked.

Silently, the two women strolled to the drawing room. Aunt Ola lowered herself into a chair, anxiously scanning the scant décor. Mildred crept from her stair and walked as quietly as she could to a perfect eavesdropping place against the nearest wall.

"What is it, Ola?" Mother inquired. "You seem...on edge."

"I am, a little," Aunt Ola replied. "You see, with all of the medical expenses from Lucia's...condition—and well, some others, admittedly—I'm afraid we're in a bit of a financial crisis."

"Ola!" Mother gasped, a hand flying to clutch her heart. "To speak of money—and with Emerson in his study just down the hall..."

Mildred glanced down said hall to the shut door of Father's study. She imagined that he, too, had heard Aunt Ola arrive and was occupied by inconspicuous listening of his own.

"I know," Aunt Ola sighed. "You know I would never even entertain talk of the idea, but it's a serious situation."

"What is it that you need?" Mother inquired.

"We want a memorial service for Lucia," Aunt Ola began. "We would host it at our house, except we fear the fever still lurks in the air. We've been staying with the neighbors."

Mother was silent.

"Did anyone tell you that you have such a lovely drawing room?" Aunt Ola wistfully drawled. She stood up and strolled to the bay window. The window was a great pride for Mother. She used to exhibit her favorite tulips in a gilt vase there.

"Such a nice, large window...good for displaying things..."

"You want to hold a memorial for Lucia here?" Mother caught on to Aunt Ola's indiscreet suggestion.

Aunt Ola turned slowly, a small, nervous smile on her face. "Would you allow it? Please?"

Mother was flabbergasted. "Well, I...I suppose it would be alright. However, hosting things like this is a very serious occasion."

"Oh, yes, of course!" Aunt Ola exclaimed, clasping her hands together excitedly. After a moment, however, her smile faded, and concern flooded her face. She then dropped her voice. "Of course, we are aware of your...situation, but if we combine our resources, Lucia will receive what she deserves. Before we move forward, however, shouldn't you discuss it with Emerson?"

"He won't care," Mother answered brusquely. "All he does is mope around all day in his study, anyhow. He probably won't even know that anyone is visiting."

"Oh, thank you, Maria!" Aunt Ola leaped toward Mother and enveloped her in a stifling hug. Mother politely returned the embrace, and then broke away and stiffened her posture.

"You are family, and we will help you in your time of need," Mother said. "To do anything less would be inconceivable."

HEART POUNDING, MILDRED stole away up the stairs. She usually had the good sense to not interrupt Morgan when her room door was shut, as it meant she was reading, or working on one of her unpublished volumes of poetry. However, at this moment, Mildred was bursting to tell of the things she'd overheard. She didn't bother with any knocking and pushed the door open.

She stepped into Morgan's perfectly kept-after bedroom. The bedspread had not a single wrinkle, the wooden floor was spotless, and the pale blue window curtains were lightly fluttering in the stormy breeze from the half-open window. Morgan sat primly at her desk chair, writing neatly onto a sheet of cream-colored stationery.

"What is it, Mildred?" she asked, pen still flying across the page at an immeasurable pace.

Mildred swayed from the tip of her toes to the heels of her feet. "I've just overheard Mother talking to Aunt Ola, in the—"

Morgan turned sharply to face Mildred, her dark eyebrows rising. "Do you mean to say that you were *eavesdropping*?"

"I suppose, but that hardly matters." Mildred waved away her misdemeanor. She jumped straight into the matter. "Aunt Ola just came visiting. We're going to hold a wake for Lucia in the drawing room."

Morgan lowered her pen to the desktop. "Millie, it is none of your business to know of such a thing—if it is true—until either

Mother or Father informs us of the matter. Now go back to...whatever it is you spend your time doing."

Mildred, although she was aware that it was a childish thing to do, stomped her foot on Morgan's precisely polished floor. She hoped that it left an unseemly mark on the wood. "You never care about a thing I tell you."

"Mildred, you know I'd love to chat with you, but I'm going to remind you again not to bother me at this hour, especially not with banal news like this," Morgan said, writing away again.

Flustered, Mildred marched out of Morgan's room, not bothering to close the door or ask what "banal" meant. Before she even had a second to ponder where she was going to go next, she nearly collided with Marley.

"What are you doing?" he rolled his eyes.

"Why do you care?" Mildred snarled.

Marley crossed his arms and evaluated her with meticulous, squinted eyes. Then he concluded, "You were telling Morgan about Aunt Ola's request about Lucia, is that it?"

Mildred huffed. "How could you know that?"

Marley shrugged. "Now, if you'd please step aside, I need to check on something in the basement."

He pushed past Mildred and down the stairs.

IT WAS A cool night, perfect for sleeping, but Mildred couldn't keep her eyes shut. She stared at the ceiling, clutching her old quilt close to her chest, and thinking about everything she'd seen and heard that day.

She found that she'd been doing this more and more lately, and when Mother asked Mildred every day why the marks underneath her eyes were growing darker and darker, Mildred blamed the stifling heat. Tonight, that was hardly a fair reason. A steady breeze swept through Mildred's open window, fragrant with the aftermath of the evening's storm.

She sank deeper under the covers and finally felt herself relax when her toes nudged something soft and cool near the end of her bed.

For a reason inexplicable at first, this frightened and confused her, and she quickly scooted back against her pillows, drawing her feet underneath her. Her head swimming, she searched for a reason for her anxiety. Then she came to a stunning realization: Mortem was dead, but presently it felt like he was in his favorite spot, nestled at her feet.

"Mortem?" Mildred whispered. She reached with shaking hands toward the small black shape on the bed. Just before her fingers brushed Mortem's fur, he lifted his head and blinked his big yellow eyes at Mildred sleepily, if not confusedly.

Mildred caught her breath and examined the possibilities (or, rather, the impossibilities). She wondered briefly if this was Marley's doing, that he had somehow resurrected the cat. But, inspecting Mortem in the moonlight—who was now casually licking a paw—she dismissed the idea. Even Marley, clever as he was, couldn't bring life back from the dead.

She knew for certain that this morning Mortem had been dead. He had been stiff and cold and without a heartbeat. She had placed him in the ground and buried him (before Marley dug him out). But she was also sure that Mortem was right in front of her eyes, breathing and blinking and with a heart beating—or, at least, she assumed.

Mildred leaned forward, shaking and cautious, and laid her head against Mortem's side. She used to do this some nights, listening to the faint heartbeats and feeling the animal's chest rise and fall with breath, fascinated and in awe of the life in the small creature. Tonight, however, there were no heartbeats, no gentle breaths. There were no signs of life. Yet, Mortem seemed very alive indeed.

"What happened to you, Mortem?" Mildred whispered, half full of grief and half full of hope as she stroked the cat's back. A gentle purr had begun in its throat. She sighed and then leaned back on her pillows. Mortem traipsed across the mattress and then settled by Mildred's side.

She stared up at the ceiling again and thought. She thought about how strange life seemed lately, and how distant she felt from everything in it. She thought about Father in his study, reading medical texts, and Marley in the basement, experimenting and doing who knew what else, and Morgan in her room, writing and studying, about and how she didn't have a single thing as they did—something that kept her hours interesting and her days occupied. Even Mother had her telephone chatting and unsuccessful cooking, no matter how much of a nuisance they were.

She was just "Millie", as her siblings so affectionately patronized her, always sitting at the bottom of the staircase, quiet and useless.

After some time, amidst all these thoughts, she drifted into sleep.

CHAPTER TWO

AFTER MOTHER TOLD everyone the news at breakfast the next morning, no one had much of an appetite left—not that any one of them had had one in the first place. Mildred poked at her runny, undercooked eggs, and scraped some of the ash off her burnt toast.

Mortem lay curled contentedly on her lap. He'd hopped up there a few minutes ago and she'd made a notice of patting him, but no one had noticed anything odd.

Marley tossed aside his half-nibbled toast and rose from his chair. "Thank you, Mother, but I'm excusing myself. There are some chemically treated skinks I'd like to check up on downstairs and—"

"Sit down," Mother hissed.

Taken aback, Marley quickly returned to his seat. Mildred leaned forward with her elbow on the table, which Mother usually scolded her for but presently overlooked.

Mother sighed, her eyes shut tightly, her fingertips pushed into her temples. "I need to address something with the three of you. With Father's business gone and my lack of housekeeping...expertise, I'm at my wit's end. I positively need more assistance."

"I'll help, Mother," Morgan nobly volunteered. "I think we should *all* help keep house now that the servants are gone."

Morgan glared pointedly at Marley

"I've just tested a new cleaning solution that we could use," Marley offered. "It now kills 59.9% of all bacteria."

Mildred was silent. She felt uncomfortable that she didn't have anything unique to offer, so she thought it would be best if she didn't say anything at all.

"What's wrong, Millie?" Marley taunted. "I would say that the cat had got your tongue, but it can't be...your cat is *dead*."

"Marley!" Mother gasped. "That was a horrible thing to say to your sister. Apologize."

Marley frowned and crossed his arms. "Sorry, Mildred," he mumbled.

Without another word, Mother rose (with yet another sigh) and sauntered away. The Mortale siblings eyed each other with curious silence.

Morgan was the first to speak. "I meant what I said. We're all confined to this house. We ought to make it a hospitable environment." Her serious, stone-grey eyes lingered on Mildred. "Mother and Father are not in the best of times right now."

"Neither is anybody else," Marley quipped. "More than half of the city is sick with a debilitating disease."

Morgan rolled her eyes. "I am aware of that, thanks. What I mean to say is that especially with Lucia's memorial, we need to be respectful and useful. We've just lost a dear family member to a horrible affliction. That could have been any one of us—could still be. It's time all three of us begin to act more like adults."

"Aw, but what about Millie?" Marley said. "She's still little. She's just a kid."

Mildred bristled a bit—she was barely four years Marley's junior—but couldn't help but feel admiration for her brother's defense.

Morgan glanced at Mildred. "Unfortunately, her childhood is occurring at the wrong time in history." She stood, pushed her chair in its proper place, and strode away. Marley gave Mildred a sorry smile.

"It's all right, Millie," he said. "Don't bother with her."

Mildred forced a smile. She waited until he walked out of the room, then scooped up Mortem from her lap and carried him upstairs.

LATER THAT MORNING a beautiful oak coffin arrived at the Mortale home, along with Aunt Ola and Uncle Oliver. It took the strength of all the men in the family to carry it through the front door and into the drawing room, where they set it upon a large pedestal that had been placed just before the large window that Aunt Ola had so enthusiastically admired. After the task was done, everyone slowly collected around it, surveying the coffin's sleek, glossy finish, plain except for Lucia's name painted on the top in a gilded script.

Aunt Ola dabbed daintily at the corner of her eyes with a handkerchief. "What time are the guests due to arrive?"

"Ten-thirty," Mother replied. "Come, Morgan. I'll need your help to prepare the luncheon."

Morgan followed Mother out of the room and Aunt Ola, with one last, lingering glance toward the window, swiftly trotted after them, leaving Mildred and Marley standing alone in the room with the coffin.

Marley looked at Mildred with a familiar, mischievous gleam in his eyes. "Should I do the honors?"

"Should you what?" Mildred asked, confused.

But when she saw Marley reaching for the lid of the sleek wooden box, a jolt of panic chilled her. Unfortunately, before she had even a moment to protest, there Lucia was, pale and stiff, lying on a bed of creamy silk with a fragile bouquet of red carnations clasped in her thin, immobile fingers.

It wasn't so much of a shock as Mildred had anticipated. Yesterday, freshly deceased, Lucia still wore the defeat of encompassing sickness. Now, she appeared clean and youthful.

Both Marley and Mildred inched closer with morbid fascination. Lucia was uncannily more beautiful than ever, her blonde locks spread over her shoulders and her dark lashes black as night against her white skin and lace-collared dress.

Mildred continued to gaze down at Lucia and swallowed through her tightening throat. "Please close it."

Without a word, Marley gripped the top and lowered it ever so gently. It shut with a delicate thud. Even after Lucia was safely hidden from observation, Mildred felt odd. Her hands found her stomach, which had begun twisting uncomfortably.

Morgan's reflection repeated in her head: *It could have been any one of us—could still be.*

Before Marley had a moment to remark something clever, Mildred was dashing upstairs, where she promptly locked herself into her bedroom.

It didn't take long for tears to catch up with her emotions. She curled onto her bed and hugged her legs until she felt a little bit steadier and Mortem, with a soft meow, hopped onto the bed beside her. Mildred stroked his cool, silky fur.

"Look what's happened to you," she whispered, dismayed. "I suppose I'm glad you're still here, but you're so much different. And I'm not sure how I feel about different, yet."

THE FIRST MOURNERS to arrive were Lucia's paternal grandparents, who both greeted Mildred and Marley with asphyxiating hugs. After they were left alone, Mildred winced as she took a whiff of her dress sleeve, which now smelled of some unbeknownst antique perfume.

The relatives and guests, who oozed into the house as the hours ticked on, were somber and silent as they approached the open coffin. Mildred and Marley stood in the foyer, keeping watchful eyes out for new arrivals, which they were to greet and console.

As far as the consolation went, some folks were easier to soothe than others. Most of the grievances expressed were sad, slow nods, but there were a few weepers, who approached Mildred and Marley with watery eyes and stuffy noses, both of which left unseemly residues on the siblings' clothing.

Marley rolled his eyes to the ceiling and crossed his skinny arms, slouching against the wall.

"What's the matter with you?" Mildred huffed.

"The matter with *me*?" Marley shook his head. "Absolutely nothing. Some of these people, however, are a bit melodramatic for the occasion."

THE LUNCHEON SPREAD looked lovely, but Mildred had hardly an appetite. The funeral party was, as expected, a gloomy bunch, most of them without anything interesting to say. The death of a young girl, despite her having been a snobbish brat, was quite a sentimental event.

"I remember Lucia when she was a baby," sniffed Miss Parkinson, an old nanny of Lucia's, who looked about ninety. She lifted a handkerchief to her face with a frail, shaking hand to pat away an upcoming tear. "Always the sweetest child, she was."

"Most absolutely." Mrs. Roister—a robust woman and another one of the late Lucia's seemingly countless relations— nodded in agreement. Balanced atop her head was a ridiculously large Merry Widow hat complete with hordes of pearls, black lace, and an entire stuffed raven. "She was a most precious child. Heaven welcome her."

Marley snorted. Morgan poked him in the rib.

"Did you know," Marley began, clearing his throat ostentatiously, "that in some primitive cultures, the members of the community *eat* their dead? The practice is not only proper and expected, but is considered sacred." He shook his head and gobbled up a piece of roast beef. "Imagine that."

Miss Parkinson let out an audible gasp and whipped out a fan with which she cooled her blushing neck.

Mrs. Roister narrowed her eyes at Marley. "What a morbid thing to say. What's your name, child?"

"Marley," Marley replied. "And I'm not a *child*. I'm nearly eighteen."

Morgan addressed the ladies. "I apologize for my brother's complacency. How are you enjoying your meal?"

"Oh, very much, my dear," Miss Parkinson nodded.

"And who is *this*, may I ask?" the horrid Mrs. Roister asked Morgan, nodding toward Mildred—the terrible bird on her hat bobbing up and down—as if Mildred weren't perfectly capable of introducing herself. She sat near the end of the table, pretending to eat bits of beef but actually placing them on her handkerchief and letting them drop to the floor where Mortem sniffed curiously at the bits of meat but didn't consume them (most likely because he was a ghost). Now the floor below Mildred's chair was littered with tiny pieces of cooked dead cow.

"Oh, that's Mildred," Morgan answered, just as Mildred was about to speak. She gently speared some spinach leaves. "She's shy. She doesn't usually converse with people she's not familiar with. In fact, she doesn't usually converse with people she *is* familiar with."

Mildred gave a polite smile to the two ladies as they giggled. She was annoyed at Morgan, however, for her hypocritical criticism of introversion.

"You have no reason to be shy, Mildred," Mrs. Roister insisted with a fat smile. "You are family of Lucia's, and I am *also* family of Lucia's, so therefore, we too are family. Do you see what I mean?"

"No," Marley mumbled into his salad.

Mrs. Roister pursed her lips and produced a low rumble in her throat that a dog might make when threatened. Morgan shook her head in embarrassment. Mildred peered underneath the table and saw that Mortem had gone. She could hardly blame him.

AFTER EVERYONE HAD left, the Mortale siblings cleared the table of all dishes and leftovers. Morgan washed the dishes, Marley swept the floors, and Mildred tidied up the drawing room. As she was finishing, she discovered a spider's web in the corner of the wall and spent the next twenty minutes or so lazily playing with a spider, who did not enjoy a feather duster in such proximity to its home.

"Mildred, quit playing around and finish up your chores," Morgan sneered as she crossed into the room.

"I *am* finished," Mildred spat back, lowering the duster. The spider quickly scurried up to a very high corner of its web.

Morgan silently surveyed the room with a critical eye. Mildred stood with her arms crossed as Morgan did so, hoping to appear as seriously annoyed as she felt. Mother had put Morgan in charge of overseeing the tidying, retiring to bed early with a headache. And just as Mildred had expected, Morgan had turned bossy and condescending.

Seemingly pleased, Morgan nodded. "I'm going to bed, then. You should, too. Good night."

On her way out of the room, Morgan turned the gas off, leaving Mildred standing alone in the dark. Mildred's annoyance toward Morgan burned into anger. Mildred had just begun to walk out of the room when she detected a strange shuffling noise from near the window. Stiffening, she turned and squinted through the darkness, trying to make out anything alarming in the distance.

"Marley? Is that you? You're not funny, trying to frighten me, like that," Mildred quipped. She tiptoed a little closer. Her stockinged foot pressed upon something soft.

She bent and retrieved the item from the floor. It was a wilted red flower petal. She slipped it into her pocket and ran out of the room before anything else could excite her imagination.

CHAPTER THREE

THE WEEK FOLLOWING Lucia's death was slow and dull. Mildred spent more time than ever at the bottom of the staircase, staring longingly out the tiny window near the front door and wishing she was allowed more than twenty minutes outside. By this time, she'd run out of books to read, was hesitant to ask Morgan to borrow any, and had no interest in reading any of Marley's. She cleaned—*voluntarily*—to shake the boredom.

Mother spent a lot of time in the drawing room, an open book on her lap, but she never seemed to read past a few sentences. Most of the time she stared blankly to the side, staring at the barren walls. Father, as usual, spent the majority of his days locked up in his study, barely escaping even to eat.

It came as a surprise when, after dinner one night near the end of the week, Mother announced that she had something important to tell everyone. Mildred tilted forward in her seat, nervous with apprehension.

"Father's store is officially closing this month," she began. "And he is very, *very* upset about this loss."

Mildred didn't doubt that at all. The last time she'd seen Father was three days ago when he gave her a sad smile as he walked back into his study and closed the door.

"So, I've come to a *monumental* decision," Mother continued, "and it may seem a bit outlandish, as very few women here have done it...but I am going to start my own business."

Morgan's brows crossed. "But Mother, you haven't any experience in 'business.' What do you plan to do?"

"I've been thinking a lot this week," Mother started, "about the success of Lucia's memorial. And after some serious consideration, I have come to the decision that I am going to operate full-time funeral services."

"Where?" Morgan inquired.

"Here," Mother answered with a contented smile.

Mildred pondered the idea. Lucia's funeral event *had* gone very well, and with so many deaths occurring so frequently, people were running out of options. It wasn't the worst idea that Mother had ever had. Despite the more heavy-handed grievers she'd met, Mildred decided that she liked the idea of regular visitors. It would surely beat the daily humdrum.

Morgan stood up at once. "No, Mother. You can't do this. Lucia was family, but anyone else is just unthinkable. Sickness and sadness are already everywhere else. We shouldn't bring it into our own home!"

"I've already made my decision, Morgan." Mother was stern. "It may not be the most pleasant—or socially proper—thing to do, but it's necessary. For our finances, and for the many grieving families who will need our services."

Morgan didn't speak anymore after that. She sat back down and listened intently, blinking away tears.

"Now, the Bishops have taken it upon themselves to transform part of their home into a hospital for the sick," Mother said. "We must care for and show hospitality and compassion for those in our community who are suffering or grieving. We should view the Bishops as an inspiration."

"Of course, though, they would be our rivals," Marley said, leaning back in his chair with his arms crossed.

"How is that, Marley?" Mother frowned.

"They are in the business of *saving* people's lives, while we are in the business of making a profit from those whose lives could *not* be saved. Their job is to keep people from coming to *us*, while our job is to take people from *them*."

Morgan rolled her eyes. Mother stared at Marley for a long moment and then continued her spiel.

"I'm sorry if this news makes any of you upset, but I feel like this is the right thing for our family to do. We will provide a service, and we will do it well." Mother then stood, slid her chair back to the table, and walked away. Morgan waited until Mother had disappeared down the hall and then fled upstairs.

Marley gave an annoyed sigh and stood.

"Where are *you* going?" Mildred asked.

"The basement. Why?"

"What exactly do you do down there, anyway?" Mildred leaned back in her chair and narrowed her eyes at him.

There was a solid half-minute of silence between the two where neither one blinked. Mildred's eyes itched.

Marley rolled his eyes. "Okay, fine, you can come to the basement. But whatever you happen to see down there, you forget the moment you come back up. Got it?"

Mildred hadn't expected him to invite her—and neither was it her intention—but she wasn't going to object. She gleefully jumped from her seat.

Marley had already walked more than halfway toward the basement door. Mildred ran after him, knowing full well he would not hesitate to take back his offer if she were too slow to keep up.

As soon as Marley shut the door behind them and Mildred began her descent down the stone steps into the cool, dark, forbidden territory, a wave of uneasiness rushed over her. This nervousness did not cease when, after finally setting foot onto the cement floor, the first thing she saw were ten pairs of tiny, gleaming eyes. Mildred cautiously inched toward them.

Marley stepped around Mildred, his lantern's light flooding onto a rickety-looking table upon which sat a large cage. A small collection of rodents scurried and scrambled toward the front of it, squeaking affectionately when they saw Marley coming near.

"If you're wondering if they're mice or rats—"

"I'm not," said Mildred.

"You can tell by their relatively small mass and the way their muzzles are generally narrow—"

"Please don't give me a comprehensive analysis of the difference between rats and mice," Mildred begged.

Marley shrugged. "Rodent education can be very useful in certain scenarios."

Mildred wasn't eager to learn about what kind of scenarios those were, but she thought—for supposed vermin—that they *were* cute. The only mouse that she'd ever seen closely was a dead one that Mortem had dropped on her pillow last month. These mice had coats of various colors and appeared to be content and well-fed.

"Where did you get them?" she asked, poking a finger through one of the cage's bars. One of the creatures scampered up and gave it a few curious sniffs.

"Around the house," Marley said. "Mortem was not a great mouser."

Mildred frowned at Marley, glad that Mortem was not around to hear the slight.

Taking stock of the cage's residents, Mildred noticed that every one of them wore a tiny band around their neck, from which hung an even tinier metal tag. She squinted at the yellow mouse's little tag, upon which was inscribed, in minuscule lettering, "La", which Mildred thought to be a silly name for a mouse; she also spotted a "Ga", "Os", and an "Ac."

Marley, boasting a proud smile, unlatched the cage door. He scooped up the mouse named La and cupped it in his hand. "I made the collars myself. Aren't they magnificent? I assumed that it would get pretty boring to refer to each one as 'Mouse 1',

Mouse 2', and so on—so I decided to give them their own identities. This is Lanthanum; and there's Actinium, Thallium, Gallium, Antimony, Fluorine, Bismuth, Xenon, Argon, and Osmium."

"How interesting," Mildred said, leaning in closer to little Lanthanum, whose tiny nose bobbed as she tried to capture Mildred's scent.

"Here, you can hold her," Marley said. "I need to check on something."

He dropped Lanthanum into Mildred's waiting palm and dashed away, carrying the lantern with him. Agitated, Mildred placed her gently back in the cage, where she ran off to play with Xenon and Fluorine. In the dim, Mildred fumbled to latch the cage. She turned to catch a glimpse of Marley slipping underneath a mysterious trap door in the middle of the room.

Mildred hurried over, peeping her head down the dark gap. Marley was descending an unstable-looking wooden ladder. He looked up.

"Oh, hello," he said in surprise, as if they'd just chanced to meet. "What is it that you wanted?"

"What are you doing? Can I go down there?"

"No! Absolutely not! No one is allowed down here!"

"You have the light, though."

Marley groaned. He climbed to the top of the ladder, set the lantern on the floor, and pushed it towards Mildred's shoes. "I have more down there."

"How is there *another* downstairs, anyway? I thought this *was* downstairs."

"I didn't design the house," Marley quipped.

There were many, many questions dancing around in Mildred's brain. She didn't ask any of them.

"Okay. I'll just be a minute." Marley disappeared into the void seconds later and the trap door fell shut with a loud groan behind him.

Staying put, Mildred took a quick look around the dank, musty room: the grey, cracked cement walls, and floors spattered with spots of mold; the cage on the table toward one back wall; another table at the other end, home to sets of various test tubes and beakers and boilers and many other things that Mildred didn't know the names or uses of. Everything felt alien and uninviting.

From below came the faint sounds of rummaging and shuffling, one minor explosion, and then, finally, the door slammed open, and out came Marley, a ratted notebook full of loose papers tucked neatly underneath his arm. He stomped the door shut, picked up the lantern, and made his way to the stairs. Mildred clambered behind him, dreading the thought of being forgotten in the strangely empty room.

As she ran up the steep cement staircase, Marley whirled around rather quickly to face her. The flickering lamplight made him look very serious, his gaze bent on Mildred.

"Never did I take you downstairs," he said, speaking in a low voice. "You don't know of anything. You don't know of the secret passage—or the mice. Not even the most adorable one, Lanthanum."

Mildred nodded furiously, just wanting Marley to quit this unfamiliar graveness. After one last glaring stare, he turned and opened the door. Mildred hopped up the last basement steps as if they were on fire, and the moment after her feet met the familiar wooden floor, Marley shut the door, locked it with his key, and slipped the heavy padlock on top.

He rushed off to his room. Mildred didn't see or hear of him until the evening, when Mother called for another meeting, this time in the drawing room. The pedestal where Lucia's coffin had rested was still in its place before the wide bay window.

"You three are going to help me with this business," Mother declared, "and it will be most appreciated. I'll even pay you."

Marley perked up at the mention of monetary rewards, and even Mildred brightened a bit at the prospect. With some pocket money, she could finally purchase some things she'd been desperately wanting but unable to get from the past few months of being cooped up in the house (not to mention her family's dwindling finances): some new books, new bows, and perhaps a box of pralines from the local confectionary shop. Her mind lingered on the pralines. Memories of sweetness seemed so distant.

"What is Father going to assist with?" Morgan asked, rather critically.

Mother frowned. "Father is not feeling very fit lately. I think he should rest until his condition gets a little better. As for the money—Marley, I see the dollar signs in your eyes—I think it'd be wisest to save it, but if you really want to buy something, I would be glad to lend you a few of my monthly catalogues. That way, your purchases will be delivered directly to us. No need to risk venturing to a shop."

Mildred's spirits sank. She'd hoped that Mother would allow them a little more freedom, especially now that they were just on the verge of summer. However, it seemed that the fear of sickness was still overpowering any want of leisure.

Mother smiled weakly. "Thank you for listening, children. You may be excused."

Mildred, Marley, and Morgan all stood in silence and walked, quietly, out of the room, gloomily parading up the stairs and to the upstairs foyer like three orphan children being sent to bed without supper. Morgan went straight into her room and closed the door without a single afterthought.

Marley turned to Mildred.

"Millie," he said, "things are going to be a lot different around here from now on. I think that, for this to work for Mother, and everyone else, we need to stop acting like estranged siblings and more like allies. Let's make a pact."

Mildred's attention drifted immediately to Morgan's closed door. Marley gripped Mildred's shoulders and gave her a little shake.

"She will come to us in her own time. But for now, we need to be on the same side. Can you do that, Millie?"

Mildred nodded in confidence. "Yes, I believe so."

She and Marley shared a quick, but firm, handshake, and then each went off their separate ways.

CHAPTER FOUR

MARLEY AND MILDRED had been assigned by Mother to paint and decorate a sign. They were given a large and faded wooden plank, which Marley suspected was salvaged from an old workbench at Father's store. MORTALE FAMILY FUNERARY, it declared, in bold purple paint that Marley had uncovered in half-used tins in the attic (what the color had originally been used for was anyone's guess).

They'd done an admirable job, Mildred thought, as she and Marley stood back to consider their work after they'd spent an hour suspending the thing on two short lengths of chain that they'd nailed to the porch roof.

"Oh, dear, it's slightly crooked, isn't it?" Mother sighed, as she studied it from afar. Her fingertips pulled at her collar.

Mildred looked to Marley. He stood with crossed arms, clearly annoyed at Mother's astute observation. She stared back at the sign herself. It was, indeed, a little askew.

"The color looks nice," Mother added.

In anticipation of their first clients, Marley happily volunteered to prepare the bodies for viewing. He also claimed to have a "good friend at the cemetery" who would assist with carting away the coffins.

"I thought as much," Mother had said, with a knowing smile.

Marley had been bragging about how, ever since poor Mortem's death, he'd been studying, experimenting with, creating, and using different types of embalming fluids that he said, "masters of the trade used"—whatever that meant. He'd demonstrated to the family (at the dinner table, much to everyone's distaste) some specimens he'd preserved with "only minor leakage."

Mildred wondered, every time she passed the basement (where chemical smells lingered in the air), what constituted his strange concoctions.

One of the first wakes they hosted in that very first week was for an adored elderly lady whom everyone referred to as Old Widow Mary, who had previously predicted her death three times, all of which had proven to be miscalculations (except the final one). She had finally passed on, at an unidentifiable age, a few days prior.

Unfortunately, neither the Mortale family nor anyone else in the greater Savannah area had a clue what Old Widow Mary's legal name was. So it was decided by the community that the woman's moniker was the title that would be published in the obituaries and written on her epitaph. Old Widow Mary didn't appear to have any surviving relatives—no admitted to being one—so her neighbors paid for all the arrangements. Beautiful blue flowers were ordered for the memorial service, and Old Widow Mary would be buried in the dusty lace dress and jeweled pendant necklace she'd died in.

Morgan, working diligently alone, crafted brochures with beautiful calligraphy and even more beautifully chosen words. Secretly, Mildred had taken peeks at Morgan at work. It was comforting to Mildred to know that the task seemed to make her sister happy. (Mildred even saw a smidgen of a smile creep upon Morgan's lips when she'd finished the very first brochure and held it up to the light to examine her handiwork.) Morgan was so absorbed in her creative doings that she'd hardly paused until she'd finished nearly three hundred of them.

The drudgery had been given to Mildred: dusting the curtains; trimming the lamps and candlewicks; washing, ironing, and scenting handkerchiefs with rose water. ("It's thoughtful," Mother had insisted, "the mourners will love it.")

While the children were working away at their assignments, Mother busied herself in the kitchen, *determined* to make a good meal for her grieving guests. It took her countless hours of concentration, several scrapped recipes, and many marred dishes, but at last, she managed to cook something genuinely edible and rather delicious.

"Of all of the poor animals that died in vain to be the subjects of your cooking," Marley commented as he taste-tested Mother's butter-basted chicken, "this one's sacrifice might have been worth it."

ON THE AFTERNOON of Old Widow Mary's wake, the first guests to arrive were her former neighbors. Afterward came the Mortale's neighbors, and then a lot of unfamiliar people. There were, perhaps, more arrivals than Mother had anticipated, because she paced between the foyer and the drawing room, gnawing at the tips of her gloves (a nervous habit) and flashing queasy smiles at whomever she passed.

Marley stood by the door, handing a brochure to each guest (shouting, "Mortale's mortuary services, folks, bring your dead to us!" until Mother rushed over to scold him). Mildred waited just outside the drawing room beside a small table, feeling rather important while asking the guests politely if they would like to sign their name in the guest book or, if they felt so inclined, to drop a penny or two into the old jelly jar labeled YELLOW FEVER TREATMENT FUND.

This had been Mother's idea. She'd handed Mildred the jar earlier and instructed Mildred to tell visitors that the money would be given as a donation to local doctors for research into a cure for yellow fever.

"The money will be given as a donation to local doctors for research into a cure for yellow fever," Mildred told an old man who'd just walked into the home.

Two coins were dropped into the glass. In her periphery, Mildred saw Mother smile.

Of course, Old Widow Mary herself hadn't died of the fever. She'd died classically of "old age." But Mother decided that since Lucia was a sort of martyr for the start of their business, it would be kind and respectful to start up a little charity.

While the mourners murmured anecdotes about the deceased and Mother set the table for the luncheon, Mildred snuck away with the donation jar in curious anticipation to count the jumbled coins and the scattering of bright green bills inside.

At first, the donations had been scant. But when the richer city folks arrived, they'd pressed money directly into Mildred's hand without even listening to her diatribe. The way they stared at her, with drawn brows and pouted lips, made her feel rather like a kitten in a gutter.

One woman jerked Mildred into a half-hug, patting her back like a baby.

"All will be fine soon, my dear," she spoke low next to Mildred's ear. "You will overcome this terrible disease."

Flushing from embarrassment, Mildred couldn't be bothered to correct the woman.

Escaping into the nearest closet with a lamp, Mildred shut the door and knelt on the wooden floor. She shook the contents out of the jar, the coins making a delicious sound as they tumbled onto the hardwood.

It took a few minutes to sort through all of it. Mildred counted the collection twice, just to make certain, and came to an impressive final count of $104.87. Mother was sure to be pleased, and Mildred felt a swell of pride knowing that this money would go toward a righteous cause. She exited the closet, clutching the jar carefully.

The luncheon was served, and although not everyone could fit around the dining table, they gratefully accepted their plates and stood nearby, resuming their assembled groups while enjoying Mother's cooking. Morgan disappeared to the kitchen to start the dishwashing as people were leaving, giving Mother their gratitude. After every one of them had left, Mother dropped into the seat at the head of the table, shut her eyes, and sighed into her hands.

Marley and Mildred sat side by side on the drawing room sofa, staring across the room toward Old Widow Mary lying in her standard chestnut coffin, clutching a small and tidy bouquet in her tiny hands.

"This whole thing has been successful, so far," Marley reflected. He looked at Mildred. "Don't you think?"

Mildred nodded, and as she did she realized how heavy her head felt. All the greeting and asking for donations and the constant smiling was more fatiguing than she'd thought it would be.

Marley seemed decently tired himself. Although he was in his usual slump, it appeared slumpier than usual and didn't have much more to say, which was very odd for Marley.

"Well," he said, after a moment's silence. "See you later."

He patronizingly patted Mildred on the shoulder and shuffled off.

MILDRED SPENT THE remainder of her evening lying atop her bed, too tired to do much else. She petted Mortem absentmindedly, feeling herself drowsing. As she did, she noticed how, strangely, the air hung with a musky, rosy perfume.

CHAPTER FIVE

IT TURNED OUT that the city's spiking mortality rate in adjunction with the urgent need to dispose of the bodies and an overall lack of resources made the Mortale Family Funerary extraordinarily lucrative, extraordinarily quickly.

In short, after several weeks in the mortuary business, Marley and Mildred were plumb tired out.

Mother decided that they were both entitled to a day's vacation. They spent the afternoon outside on the front porch step, sucking on slivers of slick ice from the icebox and enjoying each other's company in silence.

The air was sticky with early summer heat, but it didn't bother them. They had a whole scope of the outside world here, it seemed. Just beyond the iron gate down the path from where they sat passed a man treading the sidewalk, hat on and head up, focused on his destination. In the grassy square tucked between the streets romped a group of children, tossing a rubber ball.

Mildred watched a pair of squirrels wrestle over an acorn and then ascend a nearby oak tree. Beside her, Marley poked at a dead bird with a twig. Its eyes had rotted away, and its body had sunken into the sweltering dirt. A determined swarm of ants trooped over the mud-caked feathers.

"Poor thing," Mildred said, staring down at the bird.

Marley shrugged. "It probably saw it coming. Death, that is."

"How do *you* know?" Mildred was annoyed. "It might have been injured. And, besides, birds have no concept of dying."

"Well, of course, they do," Marley stated, matter-of-factly. "Animals know when they're going to die, most of the time." He stared off into the clear blue sky as he spoke. "And when they do, they choose a nice, secret place and they curl up and sleep...and they die. Just like that."

Tears tugged at Mildred's eyes. "So you think that Mortem knew he was going to die? He knew he was going to die, even though he was only a year old?"

She cried, and Marley awkwardly slung an arm over her heaving shoulders and gave her a couple of pats for good measure. "Yes, I do believe he knew he was sick. He might not have shown it—cats notoriously don't—but he was, and he knew he needed to die, so he did. He didn't mean to hurt anybody by doing it. It was just the natural thing to happen."

Mildred took a shuddering breath but didn't bother to wipe away the tears still running down her cheeks. It felt nice to feel them fall and to let the warm air dry them. "It's okay. It is."

"That's right, Millie," Marley said. "Mortem will always be around. Maybe not physically, but in good spirit."

Mildred nodded as she spotted Mortem peeping out from behind a magnolia tree and approaching her, his eyes big and sad, as if he knew just what Mildred had been upset over. He brushed past Marley and curled up by Mildred's feet, looking up at her with his eyes telling her, *I am sorry I am dead and cold now. But I am still here. Pet me?*

Marley flinched and glanced around confusedly. "Did you feel that?"

"Feel what?" Mildred asked, feigning surprise.

"I don't know—there was this...coldness...right by my feet." Marley glanced over both shoulders.

"It was a cold spell, probably," Mildred assured him. She glanced down at Mortem who gave her an impish grin.

"A cold spell in June? You—"

"Mortale. I see you've stopped being a hermit today."

Marley and Mildred both glanced up to see a slim figure creeping along the fence. It paused just before the front gate, one hand in a pocket of its finely tailored jacket and the other resting at the bottom of its highly raised chin as it smirked down at them.

"*Adrian Belmont-Telfair*," Marley seethed through clenched teeth.

The incessant rivalry between Marley and Adrian Belmont-Telfair was well-known. Adrian's family was much wealthier than the Mortales had ever been, and he delighted himself in being the sole future heir to the Belmont-Telfair fortune. His father was a veteran of the "War of Northern Aggression" (as the Belmont-Telfairs referred to it), a war hero at just twenty-two, something Adrian would never let anyone forget, and his mother had been a beautiful young debutante who was now a still beautiful socialite.

Although Adrian wasn't friendly to most of his peers, he'd chosen Marley as a particular adversary, a fact which Marley took as both a point of pride and a barb of contention.

"Yes, Marley Mortale, it is I," Adrian said. (Marley rolled his eyes.) "I see that you are coping rather well with your father's...situation, seeing as you're sitting out here, enjoying the sunshine with your little sister."

Adrian gave Mildred a small, condescending smile. Marley's face was set in a deep grimace, his hands trembling in and out of fists.

In a moment's impulse, Mildred, who couldn't stand for another moment to see her foolish brother and Adrian glare at each other in suspense like ridiculous characters in a magazine story, scooped a handful of dirt from the garden and tossed it at Adrian. It landed right on his perfectly starched white collar and spilled down his lapel.

"AH!" Adrian shrieked in horror as he swiped away the soil.

Rumor had it that at a Christmas party last year, Adrian had been chatting with someone when he began to laugh at a joke they'd told and a bit of cake he'd been consuming fell upon his jacket, leaving an unseemly stain. Never did Adrian forgive the poor fellow who made him laugh at that moment he'd bit into his dessert.

Now, as Adrian stood fuming over the dirt granules on his shirt, he and Mildred locked gazes. Adrian's glare burned into Mildred's eyeballs hotter than the sunlight that was making her eyelids twitch, but she knew that to look away was to admit defeat.

Adrian blinked rapidly, then stood a little taller and nodded to Marley. "You'll see me soon, Mortale."

He turned and hastily crossed the street.

"Thank God," Marley sighed, getting to his feet. "It's getting a little muggy out here." He looked down upon Mildred. "Aren't you coming inside?"

Mildred nodded and jumped up. She followed Marley inside the house, smiling to herself as she recalled the look of terror on Adrian Belmont-Telfair's smug face.

AS MILDRED TRUDGED to her bedroom, she heard a faint muffled noise emanating from deep inside Morgan's room. She carefully approached Morgan's bedroom door. Laying an ear against the door and leaning in to listen, Mildred could hear clearly that Morgan was bawling. Mildred's heart sunk low in her chest. She listened for a few more moments, then tore away from the door and escaped into her bedroom where Mortem appeared atop her bed.

"I don't know how to feel, Mortem," Mildred whispered as she sat on the edge of the bed, letting the kitty walk over and settle into her lap. "So many things have been happening, all at once. I just don't know what to make of it all."

Mortem, as always, gave her a soft blink of his big yellow eyes. Mildred sighed. She should have known it was worthless to ask advice from a cat.

CHAPTER SIX

JUNE HAD UNFOLDED in a frenzy, and by the time July came around, the business was in full swing and was now hosting and catering dozens of wakes a week, sometimes more. The fever still held its dominating grip on the city, and tragedy suffocated the air like the humidity in a summer rainstorm. But for the Mortales, even though they had their sympathies, the consistent income was both a relief and a security.

Mother was thoroughly enjoying her position at the head of the business. She never let her children forget that she was the one in charge, that she was the one who had ushered in every newfound joy and convenience in their lives, from the china sets she'd special-ordered from Charleston to the electric lights she had installed in the kitchen to Marley's new pomade.

During dinners of leftover memorial luncheon roasts and casseroles she'd sit up tall and proud in her seat and say, "Children, this is the dawn of a new era for me. No longer am I simply your mother, but someone making a real difference for our community during these dark days. I hope that you, too, will be able to experience something like it someday. Except you, Marley, because you will never be a mother."

It struck Mildred as odd that Mother mentioned "the community" at all. She'd never known either of her parents to be especially active in any so-called community.

More profit gave Mother a mind for expansion. She'd turned the parlor into another viewing room so that they could hold two wakes at once. Both the parlor and the drawing room got new curtains and rugs. She'd bought a chaise longue for the foyer for the more "weak-legged" ladies. When the kitchen ceiling lights proved themselves helpful, she'd hired the electrical men to put some in the pantry and all the storage closets ("Places your father won't notice for a long while," she'd remarked).

It seemed that the only thing that remained unfixed was the telephone, which remained half-fallen from its wall fixture. Mother dismissed it, saying that she hardly had time for "outside conversation" these days.

The business was closed for three days to implement all the changes. For those three days, Mildred, Marley, and Morgan swept and dusted and polished and rearranged the downstairs while Mother sat outside directing the men she'd hired to repaint and tweak the house's exterior.

After the third day of hard work was done, the group of sleepy workers exited the premises of the Mortale property and Mother called Mildred, Marley, and Morgan outdoors to marvel at the changes.

The previously run-down, plum-colored home was now a new shade of rich purple; the front door was a sleek and solid black, adorned with a brand-new bronze knocker; and, most importantly of all, the drawing room's bay window had been replaced with larger one with a built-in ledge, just the right size for a coffin. Gone was Mildred and Marley's sign: the window glass above the coffin space advertised the business in gold lettering. Even though the new window sign appeared much more elegant and professional, Mildred was sad to see her handiwork gone.

Mother clasped her hands in delight as she stared, teary-eyed, at the home. She gathered her children into her arms and sighed, "Isn't it wonderful?"

None of them could deny it.

AS SOON AS the next day, they were receiving new business. Mother was outwardly boisterous, rushing from mourner to mourner, making sweeping welcomes, inviting them to eat, and filling up their glasses with iced tea. But Mildred noticed that, when caught off guard, Mother glanced about, almost paranoid, and picked at her clothes.

After the last evening wake, Mother paced the dining room, her heels clicking rhythmically against the hardwood. She twisted the bracelets on her wrist and sighed, loudly, several times in succession.

Eventually, Morgan had had enough.

"What is the matter?" she practically demanded.

They had been tidying up—Marley in the kitchen cleaning the dishes, Morgan clearing the table, and Mildred collecting loose handkerchiefs.

"Oh..." Mother sighed (again). "Is it...what I mean is...do you think it's wrong? What I'm doing—I mean, what all of us are doing?"

Morgan's frowned in confusion and Mildred diverted her attention elsewhere. She didn't want to participate in what she could feel was a conversation teeming with upset. Out from the kitchen popped Marley, who leaned against the doorframe with his arms crossed and a smirk on his face.

"What are we doing that could be wrong?" He asked.

Mother ran a pale hand through her hair, which was breaking free from her rigorously pinned pompadour. "It sometimes occurs to me with a great deal of pain and guilt that we are gaining happiness from the sorrows of others...I know we are helping the grieving families, of course...but still, I can't quite shake that feeling...it is haunting me."

Mother's eyes had grown teary, and Mildred noticed that they were already dilated, puffed, and ringed with red as if she'd just recovered from sobbing. As the three children all stood speechless, Mother suddenly grew weepy all over again and then bustled out of the room, her tears muffled by her hands guarding her face.

After the sounds of Mother's footsteps had diminished into the distance, Morgan swirled in Marley's direction with an accusatory finger and a nasty scowl. "You—look what you did! You're always the one to make everyone upset, with your, stupid, snide comments!"

"What are you talking about?" Marley hissed.

"Every time someone needs to say or do something serious, you go and make light of it," Morgan huffed. She took a quick inward breath, and her mouth clamped shut, lips quivering. She shook her head. "I was the first one to suggest that this...business was a regrettable one. I wish she would have listened to me when I told her.

Morgan tore out of the dining room and up the stairs.

Mildred and Marley acknowledged each other in the silence, then took it upon themselves to thoroughly clean everything in the dining room, the drawing room, and the parlor.

They paused only once to put a record on.

"What if it wakes them up?" asked Mildred.

"What makes you think anyone in this house is asleep?" Marley countered.

The music awakened a certain sadness in Mildred. She hadn't realized, until then, how long it had been since she'd listened to any. The whole family used to listen to music often. She remembered the night Father brought home the Gramophone; they'd been the first home on their block to have one.

Around eleven o'clock, Mildred and Marley decided that it was time to give it a rest. Mildred turned down the gas and climbed up the stairs with aching hands and feet, hoping that the work that she and Marley had done tonight would ease Mother's anxiety tomorrow.

As she approached the upstairs landing a low, lonesome weeping from inside Morgan's bedroom made her pause.

Mildred held back a gasp in her throat and turned to Marley, who had stopped just behind her on the narrow staircase, waiting impatiently for Mildred to move.

"Do you hear it?" Mildred whispered.

Marley frowned. "No. Now, move along."

He took a step up and shoved Mildred onto the landing.

"No!" Mildred quickly put herself between Marley and the landing. "Marley...it's Morgan. She's been crying lately—a lot. I'm worried about her."

Marley shrugged. "You know that she's always been the introverted type. She's probably just processing things on her own."

Marley's words failed to bring her comfort, but she nodded. "Yes, I suppose that's true."

She immediately regretted apathetically agreeing with him, but she was tired. She stepped aside. Marley gave a nod and continued up the steps.

"Wait!" Mildred called softly. He turned, obviously irked. "But...if Morgan isn't okay, you will help me, right?"

Marley sighed. "Yes. Now, good night. I don't want to see you again 'til morning."

TO MILDRED'S DISMAY, Morgan's muffled sobs continued throughout the entire week. And every day, when Mildred did happen to hear the sound when she passed Morgan's bedroom door, it gave her heart a little wrench: a twist of guilt, as if her own body were giving her a physical kick of sternness to get her to open the door. But each time, just as Mildred approached the door and her hand lingered and hovered above the knob, she turned and quickly ran away as softly as she could, so that her sister wouldn't know that she had been standing there.

Every evening, Mildred sat on her bed with her back against the headboard, staring at nothing, with her thoughts chugging away at the speed of a steam engine. She couldn't shake the feeling that something wrong—perhaps *very* wrong—was happening. And the terrible thought that she couldn't do anything about it made her breath come short, although it wasn't entirely true: she just couldn't fathom the courage, however brief that courage was needed, to vocalize her concerns.

"I'VE BEEN READING," Father spoke at dinner.

Everyone startled at once in alarm at the sound of his voice (even Father himself, who flinched a bit), a sound that had become so unfamiliar as to be forgotten about almost entirely.

He'd joined them for their evening meal four times in the past week, and although he kept his head down most of the time and didn't utter a word, Mildred was glad to have him there.

Father flustered at once and looked down, clearing his throat repeatedly.

"What have you been reading, Father?" prodded Marley.

"I, uh...yes. Very interesting. Most interesting." He shut his mouth tightly and escaped the table moments later.

Mother lowered her head into her hands.

"That's a shame," sighed Marley, shaking his head. "I wanted to know."

After dinner, Mildred and Morgan went to the kitchen and silently assumed the dishes. Morgan washed them, Mildred dried them, and they both arranged them on the counter for tomorrow's funeral luncheon.

"Morgan," Mildred said, after a long while without either of them conversing. "Could you pass me that plate? You've been cleaning it for a while now."

Morgan continued to scrub the plate, but her gaze flicked to Mildred's for a moment. "Oh. I hadn't realized."

"Yes," Mildred said. "Here..."

She reached over to take it, but Morgan pulled away.

"Give me a moment," Morgan growled. "I'm almost done."

"You're being ridiculous, Morgan."

Mildred felt awful the moment she expressed the complaint.

Morgan had frozen, still holding fast to the soapy plate. Without any forewarning, she smashed it against the side of the sink.

Mildred jumped back, her heart thumping wildly in her chest as her sight dashed between the running faucet, the broken bits of china on the floor, and Morgan's stormy grey eyes.

Mother bustled into the kitchen, one hand over her heart, her eyes wide and watery. "Girls? What happened?"

She gasped as her gaze fluttered to the shards of shattered china that were scattered at Morgan and Mildred's feet. Mildred's eyes were fixed blankly on her shoes. A drop of blood fell upon them. Mildred glanced up to see Morgan nursing a finger, where a tiny piece of porcelain was embedded.

Morgan, her eyes clouding with tears, yanked the fragment out of her finger with a small gasp of pain and flicked it to the floor. Mother rushed over, grasping for Morgan's hand.

"Oh, dear...you need a bandage."

Morgan ripped away Mother's clutch. "I don't want your help."

Astonished, Mother slowly stepped away.

Mildred's nerves had petrified. She looked to Morgan, hoping her sister would look at her, just once. It took a moment, but Morgan finally returned her stare.

"I'm sorry," Morgan mumbled. Her eyes shone like a frightened animal's.

Before Mildred could utter a reply, Morgan had padded out of the kitchen in a mad frenzy.

Mother knelt on the cool kitchen floor, her skirts gathering in a silky puddle around her. Then, while Mildred was still standing there, watching her, she let out a choked, wretched sound.

Mildred rushed to her side, tears poking at her eyes as a swell of panic rose in her throat. She gently took hold of Mother's trembling frame, which was bonier than she'd remembered.

"Mother, please," she managed, wiping away the tears that blurred her vision. "Please don't cry. Don't."

Mother lifted her head and caught one of Mildred's hands in her own. She gave it a weak squeeze. Mildred shivered; she'd been expecting a warm gesture of comfort, but her mother's grip was cold and stone-like.

"I'm so sorry, Millie," Mother said. "You and Morgan are such good, hardworking girls. You don't deserve this, any of this. And Marley doesn't deserve all of this responsibility thrust upon him at once. This is never what I would have intended for my children, but these are hard times, Mildred." She took a breath, closed her eyes, and then opened them again with a sigh. "This is not how I want you to see me, Mildred. I will continue to be strong. That's what we need."

Mildred nodded. "Yes, I understand."

"I never knew, when I took on this business, that it would be so *demanding*," Mother said. "Such difficult, emotionally toiling work...it chills you to the bones."

Mildred felt a sting of disappointment. She looked upon her mother, whose focus seemed elsewhere. "You don't understand, do you? There's something wrong with Morgan, Mother."

Mother gazed up at Mildred, looking somewhat disoriented. "What? No, no, Millie...she's just tired. We all are. There's nothing wrong with Morgan. She's healthy. We all are."

"No, she's not," Mildred insisted, keeping her voice steady. She let go of her mother's hand and stood. "I hear her crying in her room alone, every day. And she doesn't talk to me anymore. Or Marley—or you."

"Mildred, there are hundreds of people *dying* out there every day from a horrible, never-ending disease," Mother said, her stare dour. "You cannot possibly tell me that Morgan is...sick because she's a little...weepy. We're all affected by this...terror."

"I think it's that, Mother," Mildred said. "The terror. Don't you understand?"

She felt then as if she were in a haze, disconnected from herself and the room in which she stood. She blinked away some of the blur.

"Mildred, let's not talk about this now," Mother sighed.

"When can we talk about it, then?" Mildred's voice quivered. The room was still a bit bleary. "Should we talk about it when Morgan eventually locks herself up in her room all day and night long, hardly talking or eating or...*living*, just like Father?"

There was a stiff silence.

"You may leave me, now." Mother didn't look at Mildred. "I need to clear my mind. Thank you, Mildred."

Although she wasn't particularly pleased with the conclusion of their conversation, Mildred nodded and left Mother alone in the kitchen.

Mildred's thoughts were fuzzy. She steadied herself as she slogged up the stairs. She hugged her body against the railing as her stare moved straight ahead, right to Morgan's shut door.

She didn't allow herself time to deliberate—she was already walking right up to the door. She grabbed the golden knob and twisted—to no surprise, it was locked. She thumped a palm against the thick wood.

"Please, Morgan, open up!" She kept her grip on the knob. She leaned her body on the door, resisting against it.

"*O....pen...*ah!" Mildred tumbled forward as the door suddenly swung wide open against her weight. When she finally got upright again and drew her first breath after the near fall, she arrived face-to-face with her sister.

"Oh, Morgan," Mildred sighed. "You scared me. Why are you looking at me like that?"

There wasn't a response, and the blank expression on Morgan's face made Mildred think that Morgan hadn't heard anything at all. After a moment, Morgan shuffled forward and wrapped her arms tightly around Mildred.

Mildred thought that this would be the perfect moment for Morgan to begin weeping, and that might have been what had happened in one of Mildred's storybooks, where two sisters reconcile in a tear-stained embrace and then all is right set again. But Morgan didn't cry, and neither did she.

"Millie," Morgan whispered into Mildred's hair. "I'm sorry."

Mildred didn't say, "It's okay," or, "There's no need to be sorry." She didn't say a thing at all because that felt like the best thing to do.

Finally, gently, Morgan let go. Her eyes were tired; her mouth was taut. But she did seem to be less sad, so Mildred thought that there was hope yet.

"You don't have to tell me what's wrong if you don't want to," Mildred told Morgan. "But please don't ignore me anymore. I'll do whatever I can to help you feel better. I'm not as little or ignorant as you think."

Morgan blinked a few times. And then, to Mildred's shock and joy, she smiled.

"Okay," was all she said.

And that, Mildred thought, was enough.

CHAPTER SEVEN

AFTER THAT NIGHT, Morgan exhibited extraordinary compliance toward Mildred and Marley. She didn't distance herself from them as much as she had, and she even contributed to a few conversations with them at will—although Mildred had forgotten how quickly Marley could get on Morgan's nerves.

"My God," Marley said one night, eyeing a mourner's dress with a critical sneer, "doesn't she look ghastly?"

"She looks just fine," Morgan quipped. "What in the world could you possibly have to complain about?"

(Mildred studied the clothing in question. The dress was slightly antiquated, a dull grey-brown color not unlike that of dirty bathwater. It did wash out the wearer's complexion, she thought.)

"I just happen to think that most of the things these ladies wear are unappealing."

"I didn't realize that you were such an expert on ladies' fashion."

And on and on it went, each petty subject a new argument. One moment it was the flower choice for an arrangement, another it was whether the guests should be greeted from the foyer or the drawing room.

Mildred was relieved to have some normalcy returned.

MILDRED WAS THE last one downstairs. She had just turned down the gas and had one hand on the railing knob when she heard the study door creak open. A dark shape stumbled into the hallway.

"Father," Mildred piped uneasily. "What are you doing?"

Father stepped into Mildred's vantage. He squinted at Mildred in the dim. "Oh. I was...going to bed. That's all."

Mildred squeezed the railing. "Are you feeling all right?"

"Uh, yes. I've just been working...just working," was Father's vague response.

"Okay," Mildred replied, attempting to sound cheerful.

Father ambled past her, sleepily creeping up the stairs.

Mildred waited at the bottom of the staircase, listening to Father's thudding footsteps, the soft shutting of the bedroom door.

Her attention drifted to the study. Without thinking much about why, she was walking toward it. She felt a twinge of uneasiness in her stomach as she turned the knob, stepped inside, and shut herself up alone in the dark.

She fumbled on the surface of the table beside the door for a matchbox. Her fingers closed around one set near the lamp. She fished out a matchstick and struck a flame.

The glass chimney of the old lamp spurted a stream of smoke. Mildred stifled coughs into her sleeve. When the air cleared, the lamplight illuminated Father's fully stocked bookshelves and enormous Wooton desk.

It was an impressive piece of furniture, trimmed in ornate decorative carvings, with an expansive desktop and a towering set of built-in filing shelves and tiny labeled drawers. The entire thing was in a state of fanciful mess, strewn with piles of drawn-upon papers, open books, and pencil shavings.

A phrenology bust sat nobly in the corner of the middle bookshelf, its empty stare fixed on Mildred's head. Sat on the shelf just above it was a peculiar, inhuman skull encased in a bell jar. Mildred didn't know much about anatomy (Marley, no doubt, would have been able to identify it in a heartbeat), but she supposed it was a large rodent of some sort, given the jawline and the teeth of the thing. Then there were the taxidermy animals: a weasel with its turned head frozen, and a falcon with glass eyes reflecting the lamp's feeble flame.

Mildred perused the disorderly desktop. Half-buried underneath papers illustrated with vaguely arterial sketches and scrawled musings was an open book displaying a diagram of a human kidney.

A *thud* echoed in the hallway.

Mildred twisted toward the study door, the sudden movement of her panic extinguishing the lamplight. Immersed in the sudden darkness, Mildred remained immobile, listening intently for any other noise outside of the study.

She counted ten breaths before she decided the sound must have been a brief illusion that, in any case, she ought to quit her prowling. She padded to the study door, returned the lamp to its rightful place, and went into the hallway as quietly as she could.

She stood still for a few moments, stalling her breath. The air was masked in a floral funk, like the ghost of a rotting funeral lily. Mildred strained to remember if she'd left some in a vase somewhere, withering in the heat.

Then, from the drawing room, a *bump*.

Mildred followed the sound, trying her best to muster some confidence, although she wasn't sure what she was expecting to see. She poked her head into the room first and then took a few steps in. Staying where she was, she slowly scrutinized the scenery. Nothing *seemed* out of place, but something certainly *felt* out of place, and although Mildred could not determine what that something was, she felt it in her bones.

A sphere of smoky light rushed straight toward her. Mildred ducked aside and turned immediately to see where the strange thing had gone. She watched it flit through the air and disappear around the corner, right into the parlor.

Mildred crept after it.

She squared herself in the center of the room, vulnerable to anything that might be lurking, and said, "Who's here?"

Of course, no one answered.

But was surprised at the clearness and sturdiness of her voice. She spoke again. "Show yourself."

She glanced about, anticipating some sort of movement or upset, but everything remained still.

"I'm not afraid!" Mildred said, a little louder than she'd intended to.

A strange, silvery shimmering rose from behind the piano.

"Is that you?" Mildred approached. "Don't be afraid..."

A pair of pale hands appeared on the back of the piano, and then the top part of a face—a pair of worried brows and large, quivering eyes—popped into view. Mildred watched in awe as the manifestation pushed itself into the air and floated right past her, weeping as it did so, its face hidden from Mildred's scrutiny.

Mildred turned. The specter floated with its back to her. Mildred noticed that it didn't seem to have actual feet; the apparition ended somewhere at the bottom of its lace dress.

Mildred reached for it and, just before her fingers could land on any part of the vision, it turned swiftly and pushed itself toward Mildred in one swift movement. As Mildred stood face-to-face with this poor, weeping entity, a wave of sorrowing realization struck her.

Somehow, she felt she'd known it from the start, but her premonitions were confirmed as she stared directly into the ghostly face of Lucia.

Mildred's expression must have betrayed her disturbance, because Lucia sneered at Mildred, her large, luminous eyes narrowing into a leer.

"What?" Lucia snarled. "You don't like the sight of me? Well, stare all you want, cousin. This is what I look like now. This is what I *am* now."

After choking out that statement, Lucia threw herself into another woeful bout of self-pitying tears.

Mildred stood in an awkward slump, her mind reeling with questions.

"Lucia," she began cautiously, inching a bit closer, "why are you here?"

Lucia lowered her hands and blinked at Mildred. All of her frustration from just moments before seemed to vanish, leaving sad confusion in its wake. "I don't know, Mildred. I don't *know*. I can't leave..."

"Are you the only one here...like this?" Mildred asked. She had no idea where the question had come from, and she was terrified of what the answer might be.

Lucia raised her head and made perfect eye contact with Mildred. She shook her head *no* as she drifted away.

"Lucia, stop! I need to talk to you!" Mildred pleaded as Lucia's apparition continued to fade.

"Goodbye, Mildred, for tonight," Lucia murmured. "We will talk again, sometime."

Mildred watched helplessly as Lucia disappeared into the wall. Her glowing eyes were the last to completely dissipate, blinking once, sleepily, before they vanished.

Before Mildred had even moved an inch after this incident, the wall lamps flickered on. Mildred jumped.

Morgan stood on the threshold of the room, her arms crossed, and her mouth set into a frown.

"Mildred, what are you doing?" she asked, clearly unamused. "It's nearly midnight. Everyone else is in bed."

"Not you," Mildred quipped.

Morgan averted her gaze and shifted. "I can't sleep."

"Well, neither can I," Mildred said.

Morgan narrowed her eyes at Mildred. Then she said, "Come with me," and turned away without waiting for Mildred's response.

Mildred scrambled after Morgan, who had already begun her way up the staircase in her steady, confident saunter. Mildred turned off the gas and quickly surveyed the dark room one last time before leaving.

MORGAN SHUFFLED THROUGH a collection of papers and thinly bound notebooks she had spread upon her bed. She and Mildred sat cross-legged on opposite ends of the collective mess, a small lamp on the bedside table glowing a soft orange-yellow.

Morgan sighed through her nose as she perused one of the notebooks. Mildred's attention drifted to the papers. In the warm cast of the lamp, she could see some of the boldly written words that bled through one of them. She could make out several distinct phrases ("room full of secrets"; "Why was it so?") and had just barely grazed the thin paper with her fingers when it was snatched away.

"What's the matter?" Mildred asked gingerly, not eager to begin a quarrel.

"You should never touch anything of mine without permission," Morgan answered, her unblinking eyes locking with Mildred's.

"I'm sorry." She averted her gaze.

Morgan softened a bit. "It's all right, Millie. Just don't do it again. I'm very sensitive about the things I write."

"Why? Are you embarrassed by it?"

"Yes, a little. Some of it, I mean. A lot of this is pretty old." Morgan stared at the paper in her hand and then, to Mildred's shock, proceeded to rip it apart.

"Why would you do that?" Mildred gasped. "It seemed like a perfectly good piece of writing."

Morgan narrowed her eyes. "Oh, please, Mildred. You didn't even read it. But I have, and I don't like it at all."

She stacked the torn pieces in a little pile on her bedside table.

"Well, which one of these *do* you like?" Mildred asked, gesturing towards the mass of scrawled-upon stationery.

"None of them," Morgan answered, matter-of-factly. "I'm planning on destroying and discarding every one of them soon. I just wanted to examine them one last time in the chance that there was something worth keeping."

Mildred was astounded. "But you've spent so much time working on all of this."

"Yes, and I don't mind that I did because I discovered that this sort of writing isn't for me," Morgan said.

"What do you mean?"

"I'm abysmal at writing stories, Mildred. And even worse at poetry. I always thought I could write things like that because I enjoy reading it. But I discovered that it doesn't work that way." Morgan stared forlornly at her failed experimentations.

Mildred felt a wicked sense of relief at these words; she'd always had the notion that her sister had everything perfectly in order.

"However, I do believe I have discovered a different aspect of writing that I may be better suited for."

Morgan stood and walked to her desk, where she opened a drawer and plucked from it a few leaves of paper, on which were neatly formatted sentences. She handed them to Mildred, who took them hesitantly.

Mildred glanced at the paper's heading: "The Mortale Family Mortuary: A Fine Way to Do Dying."

"It's a newspaper piece," Morgan answered. "I've sent a copy off to the local paper to be published."

"Why, Morgan," Mildred said, "this isn't even your name." She pointed to the name in the byline—Moxley Moorman.

"Of course," Morgan answered breezily, taking the papers from Mildred and walking them back to the desk drawer. "Do you think the Brontës or George Eliot would have been respected by their peers, let alone published at all, if they had used their natural born, feminine names? I'm practically begging for rejection writing in my own name. Maybe someday I'll be bold enough to be a Nellie Bly, but for now, I'm just Moxley Moorman."

Mildred didn't understand all the references Morgan was making, but she made a show of nodding in agreement.

After Morgan made her way back to the bed, and before she could resume her sorting, Mildred blurted, "I was in Father's study tonight. That's why I was downstairs."

"Well, why did you do *that*?" Morgan asked.

"I knew I shouldn't have, but I wanted to," Mildred replied.

"What did you see?"

Mildred recounted in her head images of glassy-eyed animals and books crowding shelves and odd drawings in the flickering of a lamp.

"It seems like Father has been working on something. There was this book open on his desktop...I didn't quite understand it, it was just a bunch of complicated diagrams, and there were notes upon notes accompanying it."

"Hm," Morgan mused. "I wonder what it is that he's studying if it's got him so glum."

"I don't know," Mildred sighed.

"Was there anything else?"

"No, not really," Mildred answered.

Her throat ached with the longing to voice what she'd experienced with Lucia, but she clamped her lips shut. She stared into the lamp, doing her best to look sleepy.

After several minutes of quiet, Mildred excused herself to her bedroom. She waited for Mortem to hop up beside her, but he never did. He sat on her windowsill, eyes glued to the dark city, keeping vigil.

CHAPTER EIGHT

MOTHER HAD BOUGHT herself an abundance of new clothing: gowns, skirts, blouses, and a myriad of fancy hats—the kind that she used to scoff at when she saw ladies wearing them in public— and a whole collection of fine jewelry. The past several days had seen her neck garlanded in a string of large, shiny black pearls, which she was constantly touching as if making certain that each precious bauble was still present.

"Those are beautiful," commented Mrs. Barden. She was the aunt of Anna Campbell, one of the fever's most recent victims.

Mildred had known Anna from school. Anna had once told Mildred that her handwriting was fit for a postcard. Mildred didn't exactly know what it meant but she took it as a compliment.

It was all Mildred could think about when she'd helped lug Anna's coffin inside the drawing room.

"Are they an heirloom?" Mrs. Barden asked Mother. "They look antique."

"Oh, no, I've just purchased these from New York," Mother replied, a hand crawling toward the necklace to caress one of the orbs. "Mail order, of course. I wouldn't dare risk traveling at this time."

"Of course," Mrs. Barden agreed, nodding and looking serious. "Think of all the germs that we could be carrying without knowing it. I've just read a study about how some people might be carriers of illnesses without ever becoming sick themselves. Now, isn't that terrifying?"

"Horrific," Mother concurred.

"Traveling while the fever is still rampant amongst us would be an entirely selfish motive."

"I couldn't agree more," Mother declared.

Mildred, Marley, and Morgan stood by Anna's open casket, at the ready for any assistance that their patrons might want or need. Mildred stared down at the gold chain that was draped around Anna's neck, a blue teardrop-shaped gemstone hanging off the middle. The matching earrings glittered in the midday light hailing from the window.

"Foolish," Marley sneered, following Mildred's gaze.

"What is?" Morgan inquired.

"The jewels," Marley said. "They're bait for grave robbers. They're practically *begging* for their loved one's remains to be violated. What's the use? They might as well go to someone in the family who can make use of them."

"Some people would rather want their loved ones buried with their prized possessions instead of snatching them up," Morgan countered. "I don't think it's so strange. After all, even the Egyptians used to bury their dead with riches for the afterlife."

"The *rich* Egyptians," Marley corrected. "The peasants were buried with nothing more than their name on a wooden plaque."

Morgan huffed. "It's a worthy tradition, Marley, rich in symbolism. For some people, it might be a way of giving luck to their dead."

"I still think I'm right," Marley grumbled. "I don't care an ounce for the Egyptians. And I don't believe in luck. Especially not for the dead."

"Children!" a smarmy voice called.

The siblings turned in its direction. Its owner was a short, plump woman in a bright pink skirt and blouse, her arms opened wide (or, as wide as they were able to be stretched) as she shuffled toward them, a bulging travel bag hanging from one elbow. "Look at you! How grown-up you are. Aren't you the most handsome thing?"

She dropped her bag on the floor and pulled Marley into a hug. It was brief, but it was obvious that Marley was not having a good time. His arms hung limply by his side and his face twisted in disgust. When the woman finally released him, Marley shivered and brushed off his sleeves.

She moved to Morgan, cupping Morgan's face with two pudgy hands. "A beautiful young lady. Very nice skin. You'll have no problem finding a husband." Smiling, she patted Morgan on the cheek. Morgan reddened.

At last, she came to Mildred. She paused and tilted her head, wonderment gleaming in her eyes, as if Mildred was a novelty toy in a shop window. "You're the youngest child?"

"Yes," Mildred replied meekly.

The woman shook her head. "Oh, I should have introduced myself first. I thought maybe one of you'd remember me."

Here she paused as if anticipating someone to admit that they did indeed recognize her.

No one did. She continued:

"I'm your Aunt Camella—your father's older sister. I live way up North, in Ohio, and I haven't gotten the chance to travel here since...well, *you* weren't even born yet!" She gestured toward Mildred. "Your mother wrote to me last month about the new business and told me about the party she was planning, so I simply had to hop on a train. I must say that I believe I've arrived at a somewhat unfortunate moment."

Members of Anna's family stood off to the side, glaring in disapproval with red-rimmed eyes at Aunt Camella. A clergyman had been reciting from the Book of Psalms, and Aunt Camella's boisterous announcement had quite ruined the peaceful atmosphere.

Aunt Camella lowered her voice. "I suppose I've been acting a bit rude. I've always had trouble speaking in a socially acceptable way. Oh, well! I guess it's of no use, anyhow. I'm so excited to be here!"

Once it seemed Aunt Camella had reached a pause, Morgan spoke. "Did you say something about Mother planning a party?"

Aunt Camella's brows raised in surprise. "Was I not supposed to mention that? Oh, dear. I do annoy myself sometimes."

Marley leaned in close to Mildred and whispered in her ear, "I bet she does." This made Mildred smile, but she kept her composure because Aunt Camella, would, she had no doubt, ask a million questions if she began laughing.

Mother came by. She almost walked past Aunt Camella without incident, but upon a second glance, her face broke into a smile. She and Aunt Camella embraced. Once they'd parted, Mother shook her head.

"Camella, what a surprise! I didn't expect you to come in 'til Tuesday," Mother exclaimed.

"Well, here I am," Aunt Camella replied. "I took the earliest train I could. I've already said hello to the children. They are lovely."

"Thank you." Mother smiled.

"Now, if you don't mind me asking, where the dickens is my brother?"

Mother's smile faded. She diverted her gaze. "Um, well, he's in his study, I suppose. He doesn't like to be bothered. I will make sure he shows up for dinner, though."

Aunt Camella shook her head. "Shame on him. He lets his introversion get the best of him."

No one quite knew what to say about that.

"I heard all about dear Lucia," Aunt Camella rapidly changed the subject with a weak smile. She folded her hands and bowed her head for a moment. "Such an awful thing, to see a young person leave this world. I didn't know her very well, I'll admit. I believe I met her only once, when she was just a tiny thing."

"You weren't missing much," Marley mumbled.

Surprise swept over Aunt Camella's face, but she then exploded into an obnoxious guffaw. She wagged a finger at Marley. "How funny! It's great to see a young person with such a brave sense of humor. Don't you think, Maria?"

"Hm," was all Mother said, giving Marley an admonishing side-eye.

"Mother," Morgan began, "Aunt Camella was just telling us of a party you were planning."

Mother glanced at Aunt Camella, and then at Morgan, a reluctant smile on her face. "Yes, well, I was going to wait to tell you all when I had a definite date set, but yes, I am planning on having a society party at our home. It's a good idea, don't you think? I've missed hosting such events. Your father and I used to invite people here all the time—many years ago, of course...anyway, I think it's high time that we did so."

"Certainly," Aunt Camella agreed, nodding. "A grand idea."

"I may even be able to book the best three-man string orchestra in this half of the United States," Mother bragged. "I've heard that they're simply *divine*."

"I love three-member string orchestras! They're the best!" Marley gushed with all the false enthusiasm of a children's stage performer.

"Thank you, Marley," Mother replied with a smile, oblivious to his mockery. "Well, I must adhere to my other duties, Camella. In the meantime, please make yourself comfortable and at home. The children will help you get settled."

She raised a cautionary brow at Mildred, Morgan, and Marley before she slipped away.

"YES, THIS WILL certainly do," Aunt Camella said as she stepped into Mildred's room. "And you're sure that you're comfortable sharing your room with me during my stay?"

Earlier, Mother had pulled Mildred aside and informed her that Aunt Camella would be sleeping in Mildred's room during her stay. Morgan's was too small, Marley's was too off-putting, and the guest room was still completely barren. Mother promised Mildred that she would put up a cot under the window for Mildred to sleep in.

"Of course," Mildred had replied, though she had little choice but to politely accept the idea.

Mortem certainly did *not* like it. When Aunt Camella walked in with Mildred, he was shut-eyed, lying comfortably on Mildred's bed. The moment Aunt Camella had begun talking, he gave her the evil cat eye.

Aunt Camella sighed and dropped her large, ugly carpetbag on Mildred's mattress. Mortem hopped off and scrambled underneath the bed.

"I'll need some time alone to get settled, if you don't mind," she said. "I must get changed from these dirty traveling clothes. Can you be a dear and tell your mother that they need to be washed straight away? One never knows what sort of sickness one might pick up on their clothes while traveling. They say that things such as the fever are spread through the air, you know."

Mildred nodded and left in search of an old quilt for her cot.

MARLEY WAS NOT thrilled with Aunt Camella's plan for a lengthy visit. He wore a distinctly miffed expression throughout the rest of the night, mumbling only one-syllable replies to all of Aunt Camella's inquiries—of which there were many.

"My word! He's got scratches all over his fingers," Aunt Camella commented over their dinner of cold kidney pie, her wide eyes roving to Marley's hands. "Whatever are they from?"

"Mice," was his curt reply.

"Well, I never—mice? Do you have mice in the house?"

"Yes."

Horrified, Aunt Camella turned to Mother. "Did you know that you have mice?"

"Nonsense." Mother poked at her pie crust. "Marley's always telling little fibs. I haven't seen a single mouse in the house."

Mildred, thinking of little Laudanum in her basement cage, kept quiet.

Aunt Camella shook her head. "One shouldn't get into the habit of telling lies, you know."

"No," Marley agreed.

After dinner, he grumbled to Mildred, "That stupid woman is going to be the downfall."

"It's a little rude to call her stupid when you've only just practically met her," Mildred replied. "And the downfall of what?"

Marley simply shook his head and walked away.

However, Marley's somewhat arrogant convictions did turn out to carry an ounce of truth.

As the days wore on, Aunt Camella's presence during business hours got a little tiring (and sometimes very annoying).

For one thing, she was extremely loud. It was trying for a grieving person to spend time in privacy with their beloved's corpse when Aunt Camella's voice carried from across the room, gushing over a lady's choice in headwear or beseeching a group of gentlemen to contribute to the yellow fever fund.

Her cheerful insistence on "helping" was excessive. When a weak-legged woman grew faint and cried out for the chaise longue, Aunt Camella barreled through several groups of mourners without forewarning to reach the lady in question. She put away the dishes at the end of the night, though she didn't know where they went, so the morning was a mad scramble to locate the gravy boat or the serving fork. She volunteered to cook a luncheon one day but wasn't familiar with the family's stove, so the potatoes burnt, and the cream sauce curdled.

Throughout her mishaps and oversteps, Aunt Camella grinned and poked fun at herself. This unyielding dedication to good spirit vexed Marley the most.

"How can someone be that happy and smiling *all the time?*" He whined. "It's not normal. It makes me sick."

"You know, some people would probably attest that you make *them* sick," Morgan said. "At least she's nice."

Marley swatted away Morgan's comment like a fly. "*Nice* is overrated, as far as personality traits go."

"Oh, is it?" Morgan sneered. "Thank you for the information. Your opinion is absolutely correct under all circumstances."

During these squabbles, Mildred silently slipped away. Wherever she went, whether it was the kitchen or the hall closet, she always found Mortem waiting there for her, eager-eyed.

He was also found in a place where he shouldn't have been.

On an otherwise uneventful Tuesday night, Aunt Camella awoke everyone in the house, including the spiders, with a succession of short screeches. Marley, Morgan, Mother, and even Father padded sleepily into Mildred's room. Aunt Camella sat up in Mildred's bed, clutching the sheets, her hair bobbing in their metal curlers as she glanced fervently around her.

Mildred, in her cot by the window, sat up, half-awake, just as confused and perturbed as the rest of her family.

"Camella, what is the matter?" Mother asked, running a hand down her face.

"There was something in my bed," Aunt Camella said, her voice quivering.

"There's something in your bed?" Father repeated dazedly, his voice gruff.

"*Was*," Aunt Camella said. "I was sleeping, and I awoke to a strange sensation—as if something were *walking all over me*."

Silence.

"Then it stopped," Aunt Camella said.

"Well—" Mother tried to speak but Aunt Camella continued to talk, which was more like shouting.

"But then the thing...whatever it was...I felt its weight settle on my chest. It was cold, shockingly cold. I couldn't see anything of it—except a large pair of yellow eyes," Aunt Camella said. "*It was a demon.*"

"Now, wait," Father said. "Let's not assume this *thing*—whatever it was, if there was anything—was a demon. You were probably experiencing some sort of sleep paralysis."

"Why did you not get out of bed?" Marley asked. "If you felt imminently threatened by a malicious entity, one would think the best choice would be not to stay put in the place where such an entity is."

"I don't know!" Aunt Camella shrieked. "I don't know! I don't know...I don't..." Then, Aunt Camella burst into a fit of slobbery sobs. "I'm awfully sorry, it's just...well, never mind. I had a fright, is all. You're right. I'm ridiculous."

Mother approached her, arms stretched awkwardly to invite Aunt Camella into a hug. Aunt Camella clung to her, soaking Mother's nightgown with her tears and snot.

After the fiasco had ended and everyone shuffled off to their respective beds, Aunt Camella immediately fell back to sleep, snoring atrociously. Mildred lay in her cot, feeling strangely embarrassed. She had tried to warn Mortem that another person, not herself, was going to be sleeping in her bed, but apparently, he had not listened. It was becoming increasingly clear that his coming back to life in ghostly form, unfortunately, had not granted him the ability to comprehend English.

Mildred lay on her side in the dark quiet for an unbeknownst amount of time, Mortem curled at the other side of her pillow. In between blinks, her vision blurry with sleepiness, she caught a glimpse of a grey-colored specter in the window's reflection.

She sprang to sitting, the cot's thin metal skeleton swaying. Mortem, head up and back arched, stared at the same strange misty mass that Mildred did. It lingered in the air, in the space at the foot of the bed and across from Mildred's cot. That this spirit wasn't Lucia, Mildred knew immediately. Its presence was heavy and aged, nothing like the flitting glow that Lucia had been.

Mildred glanced toward the bed. Aunt Camella's snoring had ceased, but it appeared that she was still comfortably asleep. So, in a voice that was clear, but not too loud, Mildred said: "Show yourself, please."

Mildred waited for some sort of response, for an image to come through the grey, but it remained static. She sighed, flopped down on the flat, lumpy cot mattress, and tried to settle.

She turned herself over—and there it was, the spirit in full form, hanging right over her. Now that Mildred had a proper view, she studied the apparition for a few moments, until finally, a spark of recognition lit her memory.

It was none other than Old Widow Mary—that poor, confused woman whose prediction of her own death had finally seen itself unfold. She didn't seem less muddled now; bug-eyed, she twisted the edges of her shawl in her knotted fingers.

"Old Widow Mary," Mildred spoke, shifting herself towards the wall. The woman lifted her head. "Excuse me, but why are you here? I don't mean to be rude, but I'm trying to sleep. I know you don't sleep anymore, but you are free to wander downstairs until tomorrow morn—"

"My necklace," Old Widow Mary interjected, her big, sad eyes looking down upon Mildred. "Where is my necklace?"

Mildred's sleep-deprived, adrenaline-soaked mind raced for a relevant recollection. "I'm sorry. I don't know."

Old Widow Mary's hand shakily rose to her bare throat. Her fingers touched the area gently and then curled, trying to grab hold of something that was no longer there. "It was a gift from my husband. I had it...but now...I don't know what happened to it."

It had never really occurred to Mildred that Old Widow Mary had had, at one time, a husband—of course, she must have, because she was a widow, but it seemed strange to think of, and it must have been a very long time ago.

"Well, where do you remember having it last?" Mildred attempted to be helpful in the same way she would have if she were speaking to a living person. "I could ask someone to retrieve it from your home—"

"I was wearing it," Old Widow Mary whimpered. "I was wearing it the night I fell asleep...and then I woke up here and it's gone."

"What does it look like?"

"Silver...it has a silver chain." Old Widow Mary gazed upward, nodding to herself. "Yes...and a purple gem, dark purple, like a plum."

"I promise I will help you find your necklace," Mildred said, not knowing if she'd ever be able to fulfill it. "But right now, I need to rest. Do you understand?"

Old Widow Mary nodded. Her hand drifted back down to her shawl, where she grabbed hold of a fringed edge.

"Alright, then," Mildred told her. "Good night."

To make her point clear, Mildred lay down, turned her face away from Old Widow Mary, and shut her eyes. Mortem snuggled up against her. Mildred knew that the woman stayed, but she persisted in her slumber. The quicker she got to sleep, the quicker she'd wake up to daylight, and sure things, like Mother's bitter coffee and new funeral flowers.

CHAPTER NINE

WHEN MILDRED OPENED her eyes in the morning, it wasn't a specter she saw but the smiling pink face of Aunt Camella.

"Wake up, silly girl!" she said. "You've slept in later than usual. It's ten o'clock!"

It was Sunday, and a planned day off. Mildred wasn't expecting to wake earlier than she needed to. Groggily, she sat up. She around glanced discreetly. Mortem wasn't anywhere in sight.

"Come on, we've got planning to do." Aunt Camella clapped her hands together. Mildred flinched. "Your mother wants to begin preparing for the Party." She spoke the word as if it was of capital importance. "Isn't that exciting?"

"Oh, yeah," Mildred replied unenthusiastically, swiping locks of hair out of her eyes.

Images from last night reeled in her mind like a nickelodeon. She reminded herself that she needed to make an earnest search for Old Widow Mary's necklace. It dawned on her that it was a task to be undertaken alone—how would she go about asking her family if they'd seen a dead woman's necklace? —and that made everything feel all the more daunting.

Of course, Aunt Camella had no idea that these anxieties were coursing through Mildred's mind as she made small talk, ruffling through her case for who knew what, and humming as she spritzed on some perfume.

"Would you like some?" Aunt Camella asked Mildred, waving the blue bottle. Its sharp, citrus scent punctured the air.

Mildred sneezed.

"Oh, dear." Aunt Camella recoiled. "I do hope the fever hasn't sunk its grip into you."

"I'm fine," said Mildred. She forced another sneeze for good measure, and Aunt Camella bustled away.

Mildred tumbled out of the cot and quickly slipped into an old, plain grey housedress and then raced downstairs, where Mother, Aunt Camella, Marley, and Morgan were already gathered around the dining room table. Mother sat at the head with a small stack of papers before her and a pen at the ready. She nodded to Mildred as she dropped into a chair in between her siblings.

"Good day, Mildred," Mother said, sighing as usual.

"I'm sorry I'm late, Mother. I didn't sleep very well last night. I haven't been, lately."

"So?" Marley scoffed, crossing his arms and shaking his head toward Mildred. "I hardly ever sleep. See these?" He pointed to the distinct marks underneath his eyes. "I've earned these. Sleep is for the weak-willed. The human body would probably perform better under two four-hour sleep cycles—"

"Oh, shut *up*," Morgan interrupted. "You're not any smarter or more special than the rest of us just because you have insomnia. You're such an elitist."

"Enough," Mother snapped. "It's time to do some thinking, and at this rate, the ink will all be dried up by the time you've finished warring with each other. I want all of you to be involved in this event. It will be an important social gathering this year, no doubt, and you three will be putting your best efforts forward for it."

Marley pushed his chair back and stood to leave.

Mother snapped her fingers. "Sit down."

"Yes, ma'am." Marley immediately resumed his seat.

Mother twirled the pen between her fingers. "I've already made the music arrangements. The date is set for the last Saturday of the month. As for the guests, I've written down a list of some of the local families, beginning with Aunt Ola and

Uncle Edmund, of course. Then there's the Upchurches, the Bishops, the Belmont-Telfairs—"

"No!" Marley slammed both of his hands on the tabletop.

"Okay, Marley," Mother proceeded cautiously. "Why is it that you don't want the Belmont-Telfair family at the event?"

"Adrian is a slug," Marley replied.

"Not your best insult," Morgan mumbled.

"Your personal dislike for one individual is not going to change my mind," Mother said. "Adrian Belmont-Telfair is a well-mannered, upright young citizen. He and his family are the sort of people we *want* to be associated with. Therefore, they will be included on our guest list. It would do you well to put in a little more effort to be friendly with him. I will move on."

Marley slumped in his chair with folded arms, silenced at last.

"Why don't we invite Mrs. Pepperman?" Mildred offered. "I know she's a little odd, but she's lonely and could use some society."

(Of course, she didn't say that she also thought it would be the least they could offer, as Marley had carved up her cat.)

Mother contemplated this for a moment and then took her pen to paper. "Yes, Mildred. I agree. That's very thoughtful of you."

As Mother went through the rest of her carefully curated list, full of vaguely familiar names, Mildred's mind began to wander, her gaze along with it. Mother's eyes were cast downward at the list and her hand played with the teardrop-shaped gem that hung off the end of her necklace. As Mildred's eyes locked on the jewel glinting in the noon light, she broke out of her haze. She watched the way Mother's pale fingers stroked the gem and then moved to the golden chain, and her mind staggered back to Old Widow Mary reaching for her bare neck, to poor Anna Campbell, and to the conversation Marley and Morgan had the day Aunt Camella had arrived.

The jewels... They're bait for grave robbers. They're practically begging for their loved one's remains to be violated...

Suddenly, Mildred was nauseous. The room suddenly seemed too bright. The ink at the tip of Mother's pen dripped too loudly.

"Are you feeling well, dear?" Aunt Camella's voice cut through Mildred's thoughts.

"Uh..." Mildred stumbled for words. "No. I don't think so. Hold on. Sorry."

She stood clumsily and tripped away from the table, feeling eyes on her back as she briskly escaped the room. On her way to the staircase, she passed the hall closet. She turned around and slipped inside.

She shut the door and then settled herself in the darkness on the floor against a wooden shelf, hugging her knees and letting horrible thoughts run through her head again and again. She stayed that way for what felt like a long while, and although she didn't know how long exactly, it seemed a long time to have been hidden in a closet without anyone even trying to look for her.

Just as she considered this, the door opened, and in stepped Marley. He looked down upon Mildred, quite literally. From this angle, he appeared very strange, like an angry beanpole.

"What are *you* doing?" Mildred asked him, deciding to play as if she weren't the odd one in this situation.

"I want to know what's upset you," Marley insisted.

"Why should I tell you?"

"You tell me everything," Marley said, crossing his arms. "And you're being pathetic, feeling sorry for yourself in here. Get up."

Without asking Mildred's permission first, or even giving a warning, Marley grabbed at her wrists. There was a bit of a weak struggle on Mildred's part, as she protested and swatted away his hands, but she gave in and let him tug her to standing.

Mildred made a show of frowning as Marley smirked at her. He dusted a bit of a spider's web off her shoulder. Along with the wispy grey strings, a small black object went flying toward the nearest shelf.

"I think a spider was still in that," Mildred protested.

"It'll find a new home," Marley said. "Let's get out of here. I feel like I'm trying to hold a conversation in a coffin." He paused and surveyed his surroundings. "Well, maybe not a coffin, but a small mausoleum."

He and Mildred shuffled out of the musty space.

"So, what is it that's bothering you?" Marley asked. "And don't be so mysterious about it."

Mildred took a deep breath, eyes searching the surrounding rooms for any sign of Mother or Aunt Camella.

"They went upstairs," Marley said. "Go on."

"I think...I think Mother is stealing things from the bodies."

Mildred's confession didn't seem to have any bearing on Marley at all. He stared at her, his face full of complete neutrality. "Okay. Where's your proof?"

"Um..." Mildred stalled. She felt ashamed, as if she'd just told a lie. "Maybe I'm tired, and it's making me paranoid."

Marley raised an eyebrow and looked Mildred up and down. "Go lie down. Come talk to me when you're feeling less useless."

He rolled his eyes and then stalked off in a hurry.

HOWEVER MILDRED TRIED to push the thoughts away, she couldn't stop seeing the image of the gem and the gold chain around Mother's neck. She was sure that it had belonged to Anna Campbell, and she had an inkling that Old Widow Mary's necklace was buried somewhere in Mother's jewelry box. The whole day transpired in an emotionless blur of repetitive motions and routines while her mind spun with worry and flashes of Old Widow Mary's sad, lost face.

At dinner, the teardrop necklace still ornamented Mother's neck, taunting Mildred so that she had to force herself to not look in Mother's direction at all because whenever she did her body filled with white-hot panic.

In the evening, after the sky had grown dark and the chores were all done and everything had been prepared for the next day's business, Mother lounged in the parlor, sunk into the scarlet red armchair that she'd purchased a few weeks ago. Her pompadour was loose, and her boots lay toppled on the carpet. Her stockinged feet were stretched out onto a footstool, peeping from underneath the skirt of her dress. Mildred was passing by when Mother called to her.

"Come, Mildred," she said. "I want to ask you something."

Hesitantly, Mildred walked toward the chair. "Yes?"

"Have you been coping quite well with all of the changes this summer?" Mother asked. "Speak honestly."

"Yes, ma'am, I think so," Mildred replied. Her gaze flitted between random objects in the room, trying to avoid seeing the necklace.

Mother reached out and grasped Mildred's hand. The gesture shocked Mildred a little, and she stopped glancing around absently. Instead, she stared at her small hand caught in Mother's thin, pale, fingers.

"I'm proud of you," Mother said.

Mildred didn't look up to meet her mother's eyes, but she could feel her steady gaze.

"You've lost some of your childhood, and I'm sorry about that. I see you on the steps sometimes, Mildred. You look so bored. Are you happy?"

"I'm not bored," Mildred replied. "I'm just thinking. I have a lot to think about."

"Oh, Mildred," Mother sighed. She uncurled her fingers from Mildred's hand, patted it, and then settled deeper into the chair. "You shouldn't be *thinking* so much about things. You should be doing things, going places, seeing people...of course, most of that is difficult, with disease lurking who knows where outside. Still, there are plenty of things to do."

"I'm fine," Mildred said. It wasn't a lie. She *was* fine. Most days she was too fine for her own satisfaction.

She was tired of *fine.*

There was a drop of silence between them. It wasn't uncomfortable, but it wasn't a peaceful sort of silence, either. It was a restless, hanging thing, the kind when two people have so much to say to each other they don't say anything at all.

Mother sighed and reached for the pins in her hair. She slid them out, one by one, and placed them on the footstool. Her hair fell onto her shoulders in long, dark waves.

"Here," Mother said to Mildred. She scooped up the pins and held them out for Mildred to take. "Take these and put them on my dressing table."

Then, Mother reached behind her neck, unclasped the necklace, and dropped it right into Mildred's palm.

"Could you take this, too?" Mother said.

"Of course," Mildred replied.

Mildred turned and walked away, going toward the staircase in a daze. She couldn't believe how simple her task had become. Up in Mother's room, she placed the pins on the dressing table and then opened the large wooden jewelry box.

It was littered with fine jewelry: necklaces and rings and brooches. Mildred combed through the beautiful mess, heart pounding—and there it was: a silver chain with a gem as purple as a plum.

Quickly, she pocketed it, dropped Anna Campbell's necklace in, shut the box, and stole out of the room.

AFTER SHE WAS sure Aunt Camella was asleep, Mildred removed the necklace from where she'd hidden it underneath her pillow. In the silver moonlight, the purple stone shimmered eerily.

Gathering her confidence, Mildred sat up and then unfurled the necklace, the gem swinging like a pendulum.

"Old Widow Mary," she spoke softly, "I think I may have found your necklace."

It didn't take long for the spirit of the old woman to appear. From out of the shadows the specter glided toward Mildred's cot.

"Is this yours?" Mildred prompted, shaking the chain.

Old Widow Mary's ghostly hand slipped the necklace softly from Mildred's clutch. Slowly, a smile curled on her lips. She looked to Mildred with shining eyes.

It was a confirmation. Mildred nodded.

It seemed, for the moment, that everything was fine—until Old Widow Mary's smile waned. "There are others."

"What do you mean?" Mildred pleaded, though she had a feeling she knew. Lucia had already warned her.

"There are others," Old Widow Mary repeated. "They are not happy...not at all. I've tried to tell them not to..." Her voice faded.

"Please, tell me," Mildred coaxed Old Widow Mary.

Old Widow Mary hung her head and shook it softly side to side. "I cannot do anything else to help you. I must leave."

Old Widow Mary gave Mildred one last, crooked, wrinkled smile. One bony hand clung to the gem on her necklace, and her image shrank into the darkness. All that was left of her was a small cluster of blue-white light, which circled the air absently for a few seconds before it darted right past Mildred's head and straight out of the open window.

Mildred leaned over the windowsill, trying to catch a glimpse of whatever was left of Old Widow Mary in the nighttime outside, but it had already vanished. A cool breeze drifted into the room, fluttering the curtains and Mildred's hair. The city landscape that stretched out before her was still, soaked in moonlight. In the distance was the river, boats clustered in the harbor. A steamboat made its way down the water just now, steam billowing behind it. Its foghorn let out a slow, deep, sound.

"Mildred?"

Mildred started at the sound of the croaky voice and turned to see Aunt Camella sitting up in bed.

"Aunt Camella, did I wake you?" Mildred spoke softly, trying to sound as apologetic as she could.

Aunt Camella sighed and closed her eyes, shaking her head. She brought one hand to her forehead. "No. I wake sometimes with a headache."

"Oh," Mildred said. "I'm sorry to hear that. Do you want me to fetch you some water?"

"I'm fine, but thank you," Aunt Camella said. She craned her neck and squinted her eyes, looking beyond Mildred. "It's beautiful, isn't it? I used to love looking at the river from this window when I was a girl. It looks especially grand tonight."

Mildred nodded and looked out at the water again. Somehow, it hadn't occurred to her to think that this home had been Aunt Camella's before it was hers, that she and Father had once shared a childhood here.

She felt a quiet kindred toward Aunt Camella.

Aunt Camella lowered herself and turned onto her side. "Well, I suppose I'll give sleep another try. Good night again, Mildred."

"Good night, again," Mildred replied.

She took one last glimpse of the river and then settled herself into her cot. That night she dreamed that she and Aunt Camella were co-captains of a boat that only sailed at night.

CHAPTER TEN

MILDRED WAS ANXIOUS the whole of the next day. She was bursting to tell someone about her horrible discovery. It was sunken in her chest like a poisonous secret, and she thought that if she didn't purge herself of it soon, it was sure to contaminate her.

When she finally had the chance to incite a conversation with Marley and Morgan, it was well into the evening.

She gathered all three of them into the hallway closet and shut the door. The single, sad lightbulb that had been installed in the tiny space made all their faces reflect a sickly yellow hue.

Marley was clearly annoyed to have been pulled into a conversation with Mildred for the second night in a row, let alone in a dusty, cramped closet where his head nearly hit the ceiling. Morgan too appeared as if she were thinking on subjects of far greater importance.

Before either one of them could say something snide, Mildred spoke.

"Mother is stealing from the bodies—jewelry for sure, but probably other things as well. I don't know how or when she's been doing it, but she is. I know you don't and maybe will never believe me, but I'm telling the truth. I can't prove it right now. But I am. And that's all I wanted to say."

No one spoke for a minute. The lightbulb emanated a soft buzzing noise. It was making Mildred dizzy.

"How did you come to this conclusion, Mildred?" Morgan finally spoke. Her brows wrinkled with concern. "Surely you must have some evidence."

Mildred was prepared for skepticism, but she just couldn't bring herself to explain her experiences with Old Widow Mary to anyone yet. "Do you remember that corpse with the teardrop pendant necklace? Anna Campbell?"

Morgan and Marley exchanged glances. Morgan shook her head, while Marley shrugged.

"Well, Mother was wearing that same necklace yesterday," Mildred said.

"How do you know it was the *same* one?" Morgan said. "It could be the latest style, and Mother decided she wanted one of her own."

Marley sighed. "Look, since you're so adamant in your belief, Mildred, I know a way to find out the truth. It's simple, but it's not easy. And neither of you is going to like it."

"Well, what is it?" Morgan asked.

Marley sighed again and looked off to the side. He ran a hand through his hair. He glanced at Mildred, mumbled something that sounded like, "exclamation," and looked distractedly about the room.

"What?" Mildred hissed.

"*Exhumation,*" he repeated, a little louder.

"I don't know what that means!" Mildred said.

"You're mumbling, you idiot," Morgan scolded.

"DIGGING UP A DEAD BODY," Marley shouted.

"Oh," Mildred replied.

"Are you serious?" Morgan asked.

Marley scoffed. "It makes *sense.* We dig up one of the fever victims that we've had here—a newer corpse, for obvious reasons—and check to see if the body still has all the jewelry and mementos it was buried with—or was *supposed* to be buried with. If the items are missing, there's a likelihood that they are being stolen. I *have* noticed Mother has accumulated a great number of very fine, very antique-looking pieces of jewelry and clothing lately."

As strange as it seemed, it was also fairly rational. Neither Mildred nor Morgan had any objections.

"We'll do it tonight—or, rather, in the early morning," Marley said. "When everyone else is safely asleep. Two-thirty, let's meet in the foyer. Everyone bring a lantern, and I'll bring the shovels."

"Fine," said Morgan.

"Okay," Mildred agreed.

"Good," Marley said. He tugged the lightbulb's chain, and they were flooded in darkness. "Meeting is over."

MILDRED WAS THE first one in the foyer that morning, an unlit lantern in one hand. That hand grew too sweaty, so she switched it to the other. Eventually, that palm too grew sweaty, so she switched hands again.

She'd switched it three more times before Marley strode into the room.

"Where are the shovels?" Mildred whispered.

"Outside!" Marley hissed. "You didn't think I kept shovels in the house, did you?"

"I mean, you do a lot of weird things, Marley. It's not out of the question."

Morgan crept downstairs dressed in her pink nightgown and robe.

"Why are you dressed like *that*?" Marley whisper-sputtered.

"I was sleeping, what else was I supposed to have been wearing?" Morgan defended herself, flustered.

"Mildred got dressed for the occasion," Marley said, gesturing toward Mildred, who was attired in her old mourning dress. "For someone supposedly so smart, sometimes you are astoundingly stupid."

"I beg to—"

"There's no use in getting changed now," Marley interrupted. "We're losing time as it is." He shuffled off his jacket and shoved it at Morgan. "Put this on, you'll look less ridiculous. Let's go."

Before any of them could make a move toward the door, they heard shuffling from the staircase. Mildred tightened her grip on her lantern and braced herself for a ghost to appear, but what stepped into the foyer wasn't a specter—just Aunt Camella. She held a candle and looked sleepy and confused as her gaze shifted between the three of them.

"What are you doing at this hour?" she asked.

Before Marley could say something stupid, Mildred spoke. "We're going stargazing. There's supposed to be a meteor shower. Marley's been studying astrology."

"I think you mean *astronomy*," Marley hissed.

"Oh," Aunt Camella said. She shook her head and then smiled. "Well, have a good time. It's sure to be a magnificent sight." She looked at Mildred. "I was having one of my headaches again."

Mildred smiled and nodded back at Aunt Camella, not knowing what else to do.

"Well," Aunt Camella sighed. "I'll go back to bed, now. Good night."

"Good night," the siblings chorused, watching Aunt Camella shuffle away, her candle's light growing dimmer and dimmer.

THE THREE OF them walked to the cemetery. Marley and Mildred each carried a shovel, and all of them held their lanterns, which were still unlit so as not to draw any attention to themselves. The moonlight was bright enough to illuminate their path where the gaslight didn't.

They reached the cemetery gate and paused. A lanky figure crept into view from behind the wrought iron.

The person—a young man with tussled brown hair sticking out from underneath a cap—waved a lantern in their direction. He then stuck an arm through the gate and shook hands with Marley.

Mildred and Morgan stood numb in confusion.

"Mildred, Morgan, this is Nick," Marley said, as Nick fumbled with his keys and unlocked the gate. "Nick is our cover. Anything happens, Nick will take care of it."

Nick nodded, smiling crookedly.

"Okay," Marley sighed. "Let's begin."

Marley strode into the cemetery, swinging his shovel over one shoulder. Mildred hurried in after him. She glanced over her shoulder to see if Morgan wasn't too far behind, and she saw that Morgan and Nick were smiling goofily at each other.

"Hey," Marley called to him.

Nick lifted his head in Marley's direction like a sighthound.

Marley tossed a shiny silver coin at Nick. He caught it nimbly between his palms, held it up to the moonlight, then pocketed it with a thankful nod.

"C'mon, Morgs," Marley whined at Morgan, who still stood at the cemetery's threshold.

She stepped inside, and Nick swiftly locked up the gate.

Mildred and Morgan followed Marley as he traipsed confidently through the cemetery, holding out his lantern like a searchlight. Suddenly, he turned on his heel. Mildred and Morgan stumbled into each other. He didn't notice, absorbed as he was in the discovery of the sought-after burial plot.

"Here she is," Marley announced. He traced the laurel wreath carving at the top of the fresh grey stone. "Anna Rebecca Campbell. Born May 4, 1889, died July 2, 1903."

No, Mildred nearly shouted. She knew what she'd gotten herself into, but before then, it hadn't fully connected in her mind that she'd be assisting in the exhumation of her school friend. She glanced up from Anna's etched name to see Morgan staring at her with pitiful eyes. Mildred nodded to her sister, attempting to communicate an acceptance of the situation.

"I hope you've done your research, Marley," Morgan said, "and that you know how to do this. Otherwise, this already ethically questionable excursion will lose any credibility it has."

Marley frowned. "Of course, I've done my *research*. What do you think I am, an amateur? Now." Marley pushed his shovel at Morgan, who snatched it from him. "The soil should be nice and fresh and loose. Between the both of us, it shouldn't take us too long to hit our target. With Mildred, here—take my lantern. You'll be our guiding light, literally. I need you to place one lantern on the ground and hold the other over us as we dig. Also, be on the lookout. If Nick comes running over with flailing arms, it's your responsibility to tell us to stop what we're doing and to run and hide."

"Run and hide?" Mildred repeated. "Are you sure—"

"Why isn't *she* digging?" Morgan huffed.

"You're the eldest. Let's give the kid a break," Marley spat. "Also, I'd appreciate it if you removed my jacket. This is dirty work."

Morgan shook her head but didn't argue. She shucked off Marley's coat, bestowed it upon Mildred, and set to her task. All the while, Mildred sat on the grass at the precipice of the open grave, staring into the jagged landscape of tombstones and nodding off to the lazy hum of the crickets.

The reverie was broken by a triumphant "Aha!" from Marley. There was an unsettling *clink*, and then the sound of the shovel dropping to the hardened earth.

Mildred peeked down below. There stood Marley and Morgan, both coated in a fine layer of grit. An earthworm wriggled on top of Marley's hair, but if he noticed, he didn't seem to care.

"Alright," Marley said. "This is the big moment."

Morgan, who suddenly appeared very ill, clamped her lips shut and looked away. Mildred, however, kept her eyes locked on the coffin. She couldn't help it.

Marley squinted up at her.

"You don't want to see this, Millie girl," he said, his voice soft and pleading.

So, Mildred closed her eyes and merely listened, awaiting further revelations from Marley. There were more sounds, muffled and distant, and then a slow, unnerving creaking. There was no response from Marley for a few long moments, and then—

"Hellfire and damnation!"

Mildred opened her eyes but steadied them directly across the cemetery to avoid any temptation of looking down.

"What is it?" she asked, uneased.

There was another slow creaking as the coffin lid was lowered and shut. Marley hopped up and hauled himself out of the pit, and then reached in and pulled Morgan to the surface. He brushed off his clothes and looked at Mildred.

"You were right," he said, trying to catch his breath. "All of the valuables are missing. No jewelry, no coins, not even a single hairpin—everything is gone."

"But how do we know this wasn't just a coincidence?" Morgan said, hugging herself. She was shivering, though the air was as muggy as ever. "What if someone robbed Anna Campbell before us?"

Marley raised a finger. "First of all, we're not grave *robbers*. If anything, we're *anti*-grave robbers. We're digging up a grave to make sure that no one has been a robber of any kind. Second, the coffin and corpse showed no signs of previous disturbance."

"*And* I saw Mother wearing Anna's things," Mildred practically burst out. "I remember clearly what she was wearing during her wake, and I *know* Mother was wearing exactly the same."

Morgan let out a long, slow breath. "This is unbelievable."

Mildred agreed, and she assumed Marley did too, but they didn't say anything. They just stood in their silence, each trying to come to their own conclusions about what this meant.

Mildred's own weren't too pleasant.

Nick came loping towards them. "Got everything you needed, Marley?"

Marley nodded, slowly. "Yes. We're done."

Mildred's gaze drifted toward the giant crevice in the ground. "Um, what about the giant crevice in the ground?"

Nick waved it off. "Oh, I'll fill that up for you. No big deal. It gets boring around here, anyway."

Marley and Nick said their goodbyes, Marley once again thanking Nick and adding that he "owed him one" (whatever that meant, and knowing Marley, Mildred assumed it could mean just about anything). He and Mildred picked up their materials and made for the cemetery gate, but Morgan hadn't followed.

"What is she doing?" Marley sighed. He and Mildred turned.

Morgan stood before Nick, who had his hands in his pocket and was swaying back and forth on his feet. They were speaking in low tones, but it must have been over something agreeable, Mildred thought, because Morgan giggled, which was something she hardly ever did.

Morgan left Nick with a handshake and then hurried toward Mildred and Marley.

"What was that about?" Marley asked as they began their walk home.

Morgan shrugged. "I don't know."

But through the darkness, Mildred could see Morgan smiling to herself.

AFTER THEY'D PUT away the shovels and extinguished their lanterns, Mildred, Morgan, and Marley quietly welcomed themselves home. Unfortunately, not one of them had thought of the mess they would make tramping back inside the house after spending a few hours roving around in the dirt. As they slipped off their shoes and bemoaned the sweeping they'd have to do later, Mildred thought about how she longed to head upstairs and settle into her cot with Mortem.

Then she saw Lucia.

She was peeking out from behind a nearby painting, her thin, floaty fingers grasping the wall. Mildred's first reaction was to avert her gaze and head for the stairs, but before Mildred could decide what to do Lucia swooped up right in front of her.

"What are you doing, Mildred?" she taunted. "Ignoring me, like you have ever since you've known I've been stuck here? Sure, you help that pathetic old lady, but you ignore your *family*."

"I..." Mildred didn't know what to say; she glanced back at her siblings, who both stared back at her, puzzled. They clearly didn't see Lucia, and if she began speaking to Lucia, she didn't know how she was going to explain herself.

No one had a chance to do or say or ask anything, though, because suddenly the room filled with spirits.

From all directions—the ceiling, the floor, the walls, and the down the staircase—orbs of light, like the one Mildred chased the night she'd discovered Lucia and the night Old Widow Mary left, drifted and materialized into the foyer. Mildred couldn't even count how many there were because they were so numerous and appeared so quickly.

To her relief, it didn't seem like she was the only one who could see them this time. Morgan and Marley turned in place, gaping.

Marley swiped the air, grasping at the balls of light in vain. His hand passed right through them.

"Are you seeing this?" Marley asked Mildred.

Mildred nodded. Now seemed like as appropriate of a time as ever to divulge her secret. "I've seen things like this before. It all began with Mortem. After he died, he never left me."

The cat appeared just then, rolling against Mildred's stockinged feet. She scooped him up. Marley and Morgan looked on in disbelief.

The orbs were manifesting into figures, into faces. One of them, a young woman with curls framing her face, appeared before Marley.

"I'm Anna," she said. "*And I know what you just did.*"

"Ah!" Marley leapt away from Anna and closer to Morgan, who grabbed ahold of his arm and clung to it.

"What are you doing?" He shook her off.

"Sorry," Morgan said. "I'm scared."

"Well, go hug the railing," he snapped.

The spirits surrounding the siblings emanated a spectrum of emotions (some of them, to be sure, were angry and upset; but others were excited and pleased and eager) and all of them were speaking at once: shouting their testimonies, exclaiming their introductions, and talking to each other.

"Hush up, all of you!" Mildred screamed. She didn't care if Mother or Father or Aunt Camella came barreling down the stairs two at a time. "What do you *want?*"

"Justice!" shouted a mustachioed man near the drawing room, raising a fist in the air.

"Help," cried a girl who appeared not much older than Mildred, her wide eyes darting around the room.

"I've been here for longer than any of *these* fools," grumbled a woman with braids dressed in deerskin.

"Okay," Mildred breathed. "I can't possibly help all of you at once. You're going to have to speak to us one at a time."

"*Us?*" Marley squeaked. "This is *your* problem, Mildred. *You're* the one who talks to them."

"There has to be a reason they've decided to arrive here all at once, for all of us," Mildred told him. "This isn't normal—"

"No, it isn't," Morgan interjected.

Mildred continued. "The other times I've seen them, it was only me who noticed anything. But this time you both can, too."

Lucia stepped forward, her arms crossed and her silvery hair hovering in her wake. Morgan pushed past Marley and stepped slowly toward her cousin.

"*Lucia?*" she whispered. Tears hung in her eyes.

Lucia eyed Morgan with a frown. "I didn't want you to ever see me like this, Morgan. I'm sorry."

"Why are you here?" Morgan asked.

"We're all here for different reasons," Lucia said. "The least of them being that your mother has stolen from us."

The gathered spirits nodded and voiced their agreement.

"If that's the least of your problems," Mildred said, "what else is keeping you all here?"

Lucia's stony eyes darted to Mildred's and locked her in a gaze. "Your mother has been deceitful. Not a dollar of that money in the jar you've been peddling to those poor, victimized families has been put toward the yellow fever cause. Your mother has used it all herself!"

Morgan gasped.

"Oh, no," Mildred uttered, pitifully.

"Oh, *yes*," Lucia hissed. "She has been using that money to buy herself *pretty things* and to adorn this house."

"I thought we'd earned enough from the business," Mildred murmured, navigating her words past the uncomfortable lump that was forming in her throat.

Lucia let out a small, shrill laugh. "Ha! Do you think you're earning enough money through the business alone? No, a considerable amount of that money came from generous donations of innocent people who'd lost their loved ones—so many of us here."

"What do you want us to do?" Mildred felt helpless, but she stood tall, her feet planted apart and her shoulder pulled back. She hugged Mortem tightly to her, though he was light as air and didn't offer as much support as he did when he was a solid creature. She didn't break eye contact with Lucia.

Lucia swept to Mildred's side. Mildred kept still. Lucia's nearness enveloped Mildred in a chill.

"Pay your mother's debts," Lucia muttered into Mildred's ear.

"We can't!" Mildred cried. "We don't have the money!"

Lucia shook her head. "Not all debts can be dealt with in the material."

Mildred was speechless as she watched Lucia fade away. The other spirits in the room began to disappear as well. In just a few blinks, most of the apparitions had already gone. Only a tiny collection of misty, glowing orbs remained.

Mildred shook her head. "I can't do anything. I can't."

Lucia said. "Someone must. And now that you know the truth, no one in this house is free from blame."

But there was Father, Mildred thought. Father in his study, burrowed in scientific papers, removed from all the goings-on—surely, he wasn't aware of Mother's transgressions. For a second, Mildred was paranoid that Lucia could hear this internal reasoning, as focused as her cousin's attention was. But Lucia simply gave a nod and then faded into the blackness of the air. A blue sphere appeared where Lucia had been. It rocketed up toward the ceiling, where it vanished.

Marley stood immobile, thin arms crossed over his chest. Morgan sniffled back tears.

"I'm sorry," Mildred addressed them, her words coming out in a whisper, her throat tightening.

"It's not your fault, Millie," Morgan said. "It's not your fault."

"I'm going upstairs, before anyone—or *anything*—gets in my way," Marley said, shaking his head. He pushed past Morgan and Mildred in a hurry.

But he turned suddenly, a finger poised at Mortem. "And keep that thing away from me. It's unsettling."

Mortem, offended, let out a little mew.

CHAPTER ELEVEN

MOTHER WAS IN a frenzy preparing for her party between memorial services. Mildred, Marley, and Morgan had to listen to Mother ramble on about hors d'oeuvres, aperitifs, and favors, all the while stewing over the dark truths of what was happening in their very own home.

But none of them discussed any of it. Their conversations had become alarmingly mundane.

"These napkins complete the luncheon setup, don't you think, Mildred?" Morgan asked the day following their early morning excursion. "I'm glad Mother decided to order some new ones."

"Yes," Mildred replied. "They're...very blue."

She was distracted by a specter standing in the corner of the room just behind Morgan, an old man who was giving her a rude stare. Mildred gave him a nasty grimace right back. He shook his fist and then floated away.

"What was that for?" Morgan huffed. "I'm just trying to talk to you."

Mildred had returned to being the only one who could see anything unusual, which she thought was very annoying.

In the evening, she lounged in the parlor with Marley. The house was mercifully quiet. They were both playing solitaire (Marley was well on his way to winning his fourth game) when Mortem hopped up onto the coffee table where their cards were splayed, muddling Marley's aces and kings.

He'd sighed in resignation, swept the cards into a pile, and slouched over to the sofa. He threw an arm over his face.

Mildred didn't ask any questions.

Recently, Marley had been a little too quiet for comfort. Mildred knew he was rolling the memories of that morning around and around in his head, driving himself crazy. She got him to step outside, where they sat side by side on the front porch step, soaking in the hazy heat. He gazed ahead morosely.

"What a mess," he sighed.

Mildred wasn't sure what he was referring to specifically (the fact that their mother was a corpse thief, or that he had recently been confronted by the spirits of the corpses their mother had stolen from), but she couldn't disagree. She plucked a stone from the garden and rolled it nervously around in her fingers.

"I know *something* happened that morning," he continued. "I know I experienced *something* that was like nothing I've ever studied or examined and something I likely never will again...What I saw, what happened, it's proof of that. But it's not proof that I can see or touch or share. And that's what kills me the most: to have encountered something so extraordinary, with no way to reaffirm it. And you—you can see them, and talk to them, all the time. For you, it's always real. If I could find a way to quantify this ability you have, to see if—"

"Stop talking about me like I'm some sort of...experiment," Mildred snapped. This seemed to sober Marley a bit.

Frustrated, Mildred threw the stone. It flew to the street and landed with a few skitters on the cobblestone.

"All of these poor, lost souls, wandering around," Mildred sighed. "I would have thought that there might have been some grand, guiding force behind it all."

"Well, I don't know, Millie," Marley said, looking thoughtful. "It seems like it's their choice, the people who are lost. They're the ones who choose to be lost and have to choose to be found. Anyway, Lucia didn't need to be so rude about it all. Seems like she's still the same old nightmare she always was."

TWO NIGHTS BEFORE the party, Mother was dealt with some unfortunate news. It was the end of the workday. Mildred had been sitting on the steps, absentmindedly playing with Mortem when Mother opened the fateful letter. She let out a choked cry.

"What's happened?" Aunt Camella, who had been cross-stitching in the parlor, jumped up from her chair.

"The three-man string orchestra that I arranged for the party has just lost a member to the fever," Mother cried. "They want us to hold his wake service here next week, which is great for business—but certainly not for the party."

Aunt Camella shook her head softly and returned to her seat. "What a shame, Maria. Really. Is there anything I can do to assist?"

"We'll have to search for a new musical alternative," Mother said. "I can't just have everyone...milling about in silence."

"I'll find you a new band," Aunt Camella said, sounding quite determined.

"Really?" Mother was doubtful.

"Oh, yes!" Aunt Camella jumped up again, tossing her embroidery on the chair and bustling toward the coat rack. "I'll go look for one right now. I've got the time."

"Oh—Camella, it's all right, you don't need to—"

But Aunt Camella had already slipped on her gloves and pinned on her hat with great efficiency. "I've been dying to get out of the house, Maria. Not that your house is unpleasant, but with all the corpses coming through, you know, it can get a little gloomy."

"But Camella, what about the fever?"

"To hell with it," Aunt Camella said. "I'm going out. I'll find you what you need, don't worry!"

Before Mother could comment or protest any further, Aunt Camella had plucked her parasol from the coat rack and was on her way out the front door.

THE FOLLOWING EVENING, Mildred was relaxing on her cot, reading a book she'd already read twice or three times that summer. Aunt Camella lounged on her bed, working fastidiously on her needlepoint. (Mildred had tried several times to decipher what the image was, peeking up between paragraphs, but all she could make out was a bunch of half-formed foxgloves and some words—"truth hates"—which Mildred sincerely hoped was the start of a phrase and not its entirety.)

There was a knock on the frame of the open door, and Mother allowed herself in. She strolled over to Mildred, wearing a wide smile and carrying the most obnoxious dress Mildred could have ever imagined.

"What is *that?*" Mildred asked.

Mother lowered the dress, her smile fading. "It's your dress for tomorrow night."

It was a frock dress of dark pink, with bows all up and down the bodice and ruffles all over the striped skirt. Mildred didn't doubt that Mother had chosen to show it to her on short notice so that she'd have no choice but to wear it.

"I despise pink," Mildred whimpered.

"It's a wonderful dress," declared Mother. "From a highly respected designer. I mail-ordered it from New York City. Can you not stand pink for one night?"

"Mother," Mildred began slowly, "it's not just the pink."

Aunt Camella, who up to this moment had remained silent, also seemed to share a repulsion for the dress. She grimaced as her anxious eyes glossed over the garment. If it was one thing Mildred knew about Aunt Camella, it was that an expression of contempt on the woman was very rare indeed.

"Well, I don't know what to tell you," Mother sighed. "None of your other dresses will do for the occasion."

"What are Marley and Morgan wearing?" Mildred asked. "Did you pick out their clothes, too?"

"Of course not," Mother huffed.

Mildred stood and took the dress, holding it up against her body. She glared down at the ridiculous ruffles and ribbons, which were especially intimidating when looking down.

"See that you try it on, in case I need to make any adjustments," Mother said. "You've grown awfully skinny this summer. I was hoping you'd develop some curves, but it doesn't seem like that's going to happen anytime soon. In any case, you don't have to wear it anymore after tomorrow night if you don't want to."

"Okay," Mildred snapped. "I won't."

Mother fled the room with a disappointed sigh.

Aunt Camella shook her head. "Conversations in this house are better than the opera. And I've seen *Carmen* twice."

"I *hate* her!" Mildred cried. She crumpled the dress and threw it at her armoire. It flopped to the floor.

She sat on the edge of her cot, trying to settle herself, willing herself not to cry in front of Aunt Camella. She feared the fawning that would ensue.

But Aunt Camella didn't make a move toward Mildred.

"Let me see what I can do with it," Aunt Camella said, her eyes gleaming with sympathy. She got up and retrieved the dress, holding it up against the light. She turned her head, nodding and murmuring to herself. "Yes. Yes, I can do something with this...don't give it another thought, Mildred. I've already got a few ideas."

"Thank you," Mildred said, lamely.

Aunt Camella was back to smiling again.

CHAPTER TWELVE

MILDRED WOKE IN the morning with a knot in her stomach. It lingered as she, Morgan, and Marley spent the entirety of the morning and afternoon making sure and then double sure that the home was spotless. That meant that, unfortunately, Mildred had to bid goodbye to some of her spider friends, whom she collected in a jar and then brought outside, where she tipped the jar gently onto the soil and watched the spindly little creatures creep free.

By the time early evening had arrived, everyone in the household was rushing to dress and prepare themselves before the first guests arrived. Mildred hadn't seen Aunt Camella all day, and in the hustle had forgotten entirely about her aunt's promise from the previous night. When she opened her wardrobe's doors to take out the dreaded dress, she was surprised at what she found.

Though it remained an awful menagerie of pink, the hideous bows were gone, and the long, ruffled sleeves had been cut to elbow length. The skirt had been hemmed shorter, and the neckline, sleeves, and waist were newly trimmed in black silk. It was, altogether, much less offensive.

Pinned to the collar was a note, written in a large, neat scrawl:

I couldn't do much, given the time frame, but I think I took care of the worst.

After she wriggled herself into the dress, Mildred headed down the staircase. Mother absentmindedly paced the foyer. She saw Mildred barreling towards her and paused.

"Oh, Mildred! Good, I was expecting you," she said.

Mildred anticipated Mother to comment on the altered state of her dress. Instead, she asked, "Have you seen my necklace, the one with the purple stone? I wore it sometime last week, I think..."

"No, I haven't seen it," Mildred replied, steadily meeting Mother's eyes.

"Oh," Mother sighed. "It goes so perfectly with my gown." Her brows crossed. She gazed at Mildred's attire, a flash of confusion crossing her face, but then she shook her head. "I suppose I'll have to find something else to wear tonight."

She gathered her skirts and bustled up the staircase. When she came back downstairs, she wore a black diamond choker. (Mildred wondered at its origins.)

Aunt Camella then descended the stairs, adorned in a lavender ballgown, a feathered hat balanced precariously atop her curled hair.

"Camella, how nice you look!" Mother gushed.

"Why, thank you." Aunt Camella smiled.

Father moseyed into the foyer, a book tucked underneath one arm. He squinted up at Aunt Camella. "What's with the feathers?"

"What's with *this*?" Mother screeched.

She pulled the book away from him, pinching it between her fingers. "This is unacceptable, Emerson. I'm putting this away for now. You'll get it back tonight after the party is over."

Mother stomped away. She returned several minutes later, bookless and smug.

Mildred twitched uncomfortably as she stood in the foyer with Mother, Father, and Aunt Camella, anxious for either Morgan or Marley to appear.

"Mildred, would you please stop with the fidgeting," Mother scolded. "It's making me cringe."

"Sorry," Mildred barely mumbled, rolling her shoulders back, trying to loosen the stiff, starchy material of the dress.

"Now, where are your siblings?" Mother sighed.

Mildred took up the staircase, calling out behind her, "I'll get Morgan!"

She skipped up the last of the steps two at a time, knocked a few times curtly on Morgan's door, and then let herself inside. Morgan sat in front of her vanity, staring at herself gloomily in the mirror. Mildred shut the door gently and crept forward. Mildred could see herself plainly in the vanity's reflection, but Morgan's gaze did not lift from her own likeness.

Mildred laid a hand on Morgan's shoulder. Morgan flinched at her touch. "Mildred...what is it?"

"Mother wants you downstairs."

Morgan pursed her lips and looked down. "Oh, Mildred, I don't want to have this party. Do you?"

"Not really."

"The thought of so many people in the house all at once makes me uneasy." Morgan tucked a loose curl behind her ear, her hand trembling.

"But people—strangers—are in our house all the time," Mildred said.

"Yes, Mildred, but most of them are dead—or half-alive with grief."

Mildred couldn't disagree. She shifted her weight from one foot to the other. "You know, no one knows where Marley is—"

Morgan scowled. "Oh, that idiot."

Morgan flattened her palms on the surface of her vanity and pushed herself up. She rushed past Mildred.

Mildred stumbled after her. "You know where he is, then?"

Mildred scurried down the staircase after Morgan, who marched on as forward and focused as an army general.

"Oh, there you are," Mother said, as the girls approached. "Let me take a look at you—now, where are you going?"

Mother bustled after them, following Morgan through the front door. Father and Aunt Camella trailed reluctantly at Mother's heels. Outside, Morgan walked to a spot within a reasonable view of the home and then pointed upwards.

Everyone looked up.

"I heard him up there while I was getting ready," Morgan said. "He was threatening some pigeons."

Mildred squinted into the burning sunlight. She could make out a slim figure atop the house, looming from the widow's walk.

"MARLEY!" Mother screamed. "GET DOWN FROM THERE!"

There was no answer from above. Mother looked to Mildred and Morgan.

"Get him. *Now.*"

Obediently, they rushed inside and made their way up. The moment they clambered to the rooftop, Marley spun to face them.

"What are you doing?" Mildred demanded.

"I'm watching out for that toad Adrian Belmont-Telfair," Marley was quick to answer.

"Well, he's on his way and there's nothing you can do about it," Morgan huffed. "You look ridiculous up here, by the way."

Marley shook his head and tweaked the purple ascot at his neck. His hair was slickly parted, and he wore a purple waistcoat and pristine black jacket, and silver cufflinks. Though Mildred had a mind to compliment him, she knew better than to indulge his comfortable conceit.

"Your ascot is crooked," she said. (It was.)

"I *know*," he scoffed.

He made no effort to straighten it.

THERE WAS A knock at the door unexpectedly early. Mother froze in a white-faced panic. No one spoke as she strode to the door and swung it open.

There stood three formally attired men: one with a cello, one with a violin, and one with an upright bass.

Silence ensued.

"This is the Mortale residence, yes?" the violinist asked.

"Yes," Mother said. She shook her head. "Sorry, I was under the impression that one of you had..."

"Yes, Frederic died three days ago," the bassist said. The three of them bowed their heads momentarily. "But we found a replacement."

The cellist raised a hand.

"Oh," Mother replied. "Well, come in. I apologize for the misunderstanding. Please, follow me..."

Mother held the door open for them. Once they'd wrangled their instruments inside, she led them into the parlor to set up.

Aunt Camella had suddenly become very flustered. She whipped out a feathered fan.

"Oh, dear," she breathed. "Oh dear, oh dear, oh dear..."

"What is it?" Marley hissed.

"It's just that I...the band I found—the replacement band, you see—they're not like that at *all*."

She fanned more enthusiastically.

There was another knock. Mother came dashing from the parlor to the door. She opened it to the smiling faces of Mr. and Mrs. Upchurch, whom she greeted excitedly and then presented to Father. She was so pleased with the arrival of the first guests that she didn't even ask why they'd shown up thirty minutes early.

After the Upchurches had made a customary round of greetings to the adults, Mr. Upchurch followed Father to the parlor for drinks and Mrs. Upchurch assailed the children. She went for Mildred first, leaning it for a quick, half-hearted embrace. She smelled overwhelmingly floral, like funeral flower arrangements in the midday sun. It turned Mildred's stomach.

"How do you do?" Mrs. Upchurch asked, flashing her pearly teeth.

"I'm well," Mildred replied politely, reminding herself to smile.

"Very well," Mrs. Upchurch said and turned to Morgan. "And you?"

"I'm fine, thank you," Morgan replied.

Mrs. Upchurch nodded, then turned to Marley. "And this is your brother, I presume?"

Marley gave her a close-lipped smile. "I believe your perfume is baby's breath."

Mrs. Upchurch seemed pleasantly surprised. "Why, yes, it is!"

"Funny thing, baby's breath." Marley shook his head. "The name is so deceivingly innocent. The entire plant is highly toxic, and if ingested can trigger excessive vomiting, not unlike the yellow fever that's been going around."

Mrs. Upchurch's smile diminished to an ugly curl of the lips. "Thank you. Now, where is your powder room?"

Without waiting for an answer, the lady rushed to locate her husband.

Aunt Ola and Uncle Edmund arrived, met with kisses from Mother and Aunt Camella. Their interaction was broken when the front door burst open and in tramped a trio of young people, all laughing as if they'd just heard the most delightful thing in the world.

"Oh my," Aunt Ola breathed.

Uncle Edmund cleared his throat noisily.

"Hello," Mother said steadily, "what is this?"

Aunt Camella shuffled over sheepishly. "This is the replacement band I found for you, Maria."

The group consisted of two young women and a boy who appeared to be about Marley's age. The girls wore the most appalling dresses Mildred had ever seen, all lopsided and tattered. One of the girls' dresses looked as if it had been white once—but now it was an off-cream hue, spotted in tea-colored stains. The other girl's dress, a surprisingly pleasant shade of blue, fell loose on one side of her body, exposing a bare shoulder. Both wore their hair piled in loose bundles atop their heads. The boy wore a button-up shirt of the same dirtied white as the one girl's dress, sleeves half-rolled, tucked into patched brown trousers. Skewed upon his head was what looked like a soldier's cap with the emblem removed.

The girl in the blue dress raised her instrument, a scuffed violin with different colored strings. "So, where are we playin' at?"

Mother was stunned. "I...I suppose in that room, over there, the drawing room. The...other band...has the parlor."

"I'm so sorry, Maria," Aunt Camella said, "they were just so talented...wait until you hear them play..."

"What exactly do you play?" Mother asked them.

"Fiddle," the girl in the blue dress said with a smile.

"Banjo," said the girl in stained white.

"Spoons," said the boy.

"You can play...spoons?"

The doorbell rang. Mother smoothed down her sleeves and rolled back her shoulders. She sighed at Aunt Camella.

"I'm sorry, but I can't deal with this any longer. I must assume the role of hostess."

The girl in the stained dress shrugged and marched toward the drawing room. Her bandmates followed.

Aunt Camella looked positively mortified. "I've ruined the night, haven't I?"

"Oh, no," Mildred reassured her. "The group you invited seems a lot more interesting than those professionals."

"I can't wait to hear what they sound like," Mildred added.

Marley gently steered Aunt Camella away from the gathering in the foyer. "Why don't you get yourself a glass of punch, Aunt Camella? There's some over in the dining room."

"Yes, that's a very good suggestion, Marley," Aunt Camella said.

She cheerily went to fetch a glass.

After that, it seemed to Mildred that at every turn she was forced into the acquaintance of stylishly dressed adults, most of whom spoke to her in the same smarmy tone. Morgan had been by her side for a while until she managed to slip away to a quiet spot in the drawing room with a finger sandwich and glass of Chatham Artillery punch. Mildred could see her plainly over the shoulder of some woman who claimed to be Mother's oldest friend, chomping away at the thin bread.

In her peripheral, Mildred saw Mrs. Pepperman ambling confusedly through the foyer crowd. Mildred excused herself from the woman talking at her and swept to Mrs. Pepperman's side. Mildred greeted her warmly and guided the lady by one of her thin arms. Mrs. Pepperman patted Mildred's hand and looked upon the scenery with delight.

She glanced at Mildred with her slightly buggy eyes and asked, hopefully, "Is this where Salty is?"

"Oh, no," Mildred shook her head. "But he might be in the kitchen. You know how he likes his scraps."

Mrs. Pepperman nodded, seemingly pleased by that. "Oh, but it's 'she.' But I wouldn't have expected you to know that, honey. I'm just glad someone is keeping her fed. You know, the day she disappeared, a strange-looking dark-haired boy was sneaking around my garden." Mrs. Pepperman slowed, squinting ahead. "Why, there he is!"

Mildred followed Mrs. Pepperman's gaze, which landed on Marley. Mildred tugged Mrs. Pepperman away as the lady muttered, "How odd", again and again under her breath.

It was about this time when the three-man string band caused a bit of a scene by packing up and marching to the foyer. Mother, who had been having a serious conversation about floral arrangements with Mrs. Upchurch, was startled to see them rushing at her.

"Hello, gentlemen," she said. "Whatever is the matter?"

"We cannot tune our instruments with that...gang of orphans in the other room," snarled the cellist. "We can barely focus with all the noise they're making."

"Oh, I don't think they're orphans." Mother smiled. "I think they're just homeless."

From the drawing room began another loud and lively folk song, accompanied by stomping and hollering. Some guests had gathered near the threshold to watch, enthralled and amused.

The musicians standing in the foyer were not.

"Good night, Mrs. Mortale," the violinist said. "We will see on Tuesday for Frederic's wake."

The three of them immediately made for the door.

MARLEY HAD BEEN drawn into a conversation with the dreaded Mrs. Roister. She donned another one of her horrible hats adorned with a whole bird. Her glassy eyes bore down upon him as she awaited his response to her accusation and subsequent question ("Ah, I remember you, young man. You had such smart things to say. What have you been occupying yourself with lately?").

Marley nodded to her hat. "I like your pigeon."

Mrs. Roister frowned. "It's a dove."

"So is a pigeon."

"How old you did say you were, again?" she asked him.

"I'm sorry, I can't hear you over the sound of the spoons!" shouted Marley.

"How old did you say you were, again?" Mrs. Roister repeated, her throat straining against her collar.

"I'm almost eighteen," Marley replied.

Mrs. Roister smirked. "Seventeen years old...do you have any career plans? Are you going into the family business?"

"If by 'family business,' you mean 'mortuary science,' sure, I could do that," Marley replied. "I've taught myself extensively in the subject of thanatology. But I like to think bigger than that. Haven't you heard of paleometatomology?"

Mrs. Roister shook her head. Her pigeon bobbed.

"It's an extremely absorbing subject," Marley said. "Really something."

"Well, what is it?" Mrs. Roister tilted her head.

"It's the study of idiocy."

"Idiocy...?"

"Oh, yes. All aspects of it. There's quite a lot to study here tonight."

"Certainly." Mrs. Roister lifted her chin. "You'll have to tell me the discoveries of your...study the next time we meet. I am a hobbyist in the sciences myself—domestic sciences, you know."

Mildred had watched the entire exchange from across the way, leaning against the wallpaper with Mrs. Pepperman beside her, happily occupied with a plateful of stuffed olives.

The music was suspended as the band passed around a pitcher of punch. But the air was charged with a hush besides: in had walked Adrian Belmont-Telfair and his parents, all of them as proud and polished as they'd ever been.

Mildred rushed to Marley.

"Pardon me, Mrs. Roister," Marley told her. "My little sister is begging for my attention."

Before waiting for a reply from Mrs. Roister, he turned and fairly ran away. Mildred took after him. He seemed to have forgotten that she'd wanted to speak to him because he turned abruptly and smashed right into her.

"What is it?" he hissed.

"*Look.*"

At once, Marley's head jerked up. He emanated a low rumble, not unlike that of an annoyed cat. "I see him, the leech."

The leech saw him as well because the Belmont-Telfairs were now headed in their direction. Marley stiffened but contained his composure. Mildred slunk behind her brother's tall frame, which wasn't much help at all because he was so thin.

Adrian's face lit with a cheeky smile as he strolled to them, his parents behind him on either side.

"Good evening, Marley," Adrian snarled.

"It was," said Marley.

Mr. Belmont-Telfair roared with laughter and patted Adrian on the back. "You boys are so funny. Aren't they, darling?"

"Yes, very funny, indeed," agreed Mrs. Belmont-Telfair. She flashed her pursed pink lips in Marley's direction. Mildred scrutinized her from behind Marley, taking in her impeccable ash-blonde ringlets and cool blue eyes, the very same as Adrian's.

She caught Mildred's stare. Her brows lifted in surprise.

"Who is *that?*" she cooed.

Mildred stepped aside. She imagined that her cheeks blushed as pink as her clothes.

"You're Marley's little sister, aren't you? I don't think we've been acquainted."

"No," Mildred replied.

Adrian stared down Mildred. "That's the little waif who tossed dirt at me."

Both of Adrian's parents laughed in cheerful volumes.

Mrs. Belmont-Telfair laid a hand on her son's shoulder. She pressed a quick kiss to the side of his head, and then she and her husband strode away, arm in arm.

Adrian tilted his head at Marley. "This is a very interesting party, Mortale. And such *horrendous* entertainment. I'm assuming you had something to do with *this* band of delinquents."

From the far side of the room, the girl with the banjo catapulted into a high-spirited solo.

"Disappointingly, no," Marley said.

Adrian scoffed in disbelief. His focus then snapped to Mildred. "What's the matter with *you?* I've hardly seen a more repulsive color of pink than the kind you're wearing."

"My mother made me wear it," mumbled Mildred.

Adrian smirked. "It was in poor taste."

"Adrian, shut your mouth," Marley snapped.

Adrian gave an apathetic shrug and wandered off.

"Go waste your energy elsewhere!" Marley shouted after him.

Adrian glanced over his shoulder with a sneer.

Mildred shook her head. "What an insignificant slug."

"You've never said anything truer," Marley sighed.

Aunt Camella came bustling toward them just then, shouting their names. One hand grasped her layered skirt and the other supported a glass of punch, which sloshed dangerously as she staggered forward.

"There you are," Aunt Camella huffed, coming to a stop at last. She took a long drink from her glass.

"Aunt Camella," Mildred began, hesitantly, "how many glasses of punch have you drunk?"

"Oh, I don't know," Aunt Camella breathed. "Only two...maybe three? It's very, *very* good." She fumbled with the fan hanging from her wrist. She tugged at her lace collar and exhaled dramatically. "It is a bit humid in here, isn't it? Oh, and did you see Morgan? She's with a gentleman over by that strange group of musical hooligans." She leaned in closer. Mildred was enveloped in a sour, warm breath. "He's a bit weird looking, but strangely not unappealing."

Aunt Camella giggled, then hiccoughed.

Marley and Mildred glanced over their shoulders: there was Morgan, standing beside the hoodlum band, engaged in what seemed like a pleasant conversation with Nick from the cemetery.

"You bastard," Marley practically shouted at him as he led Mildred and Aunt Camella through the room. "You didn't even tell me you were going to be here."

Morgan huffed and crossed her arms.

"Wait, why is he here?" Mildred asked.

"Nick is of the *Dobson* family, Mildred," Morgan answered.

Mildred shook her head. Morgan rolled her eyes.

"They're ship merchants. They own practically every vessel in the harbor."

"Why does he work in the cemetery, then?" asked Mildred.

Nick shrugged. "Builds character."

"Oh, you're being so *loud!*" Aunt Camella screeched at the band, clamping both of her hands (including the one precariously clutching the punch glass) to her ears.

Mildred and Marley reached for Aunt Camella, steadying her. When they grasped her by the arm on either side, Aunt Camella glanced between them.

"Am I going someplace?"

"To lie down for a bit," Marley said.

"Ah, that sounds nice," Aunt Camella gushed.

They walked her to the chaise longue. Giggling the whole way, Aunt Camella's head kept flopping onto Mildred's shoulder.

"Oh, you are so *nice*, Mildred," Aunt Camella burbled. "Old Widow Mary was right about you."

Mildred paused. Aunt Camella stumbled forward. Marley reeled her in.

"Aunt Camella, what did you just say?"

"Old Mary Widow," Aunt Camella said, mixing up her words. "You know her?"

"Yes," Mildred said. "What did she say to you? When did you talk to her?"

Aunt Camella shook her head. "Oh, dear. There I go, gabbing about nonsense. You know me, Mildred."

They deposited Aunt Camella gently onto the chaise longue. Mildred slipped the glass from Aunt Camella's hand and Marley tucked a decorative pillow underneath her head. Aunt Camella snuggled into the pillow's beaded design and her eyes fluttered shut.

As Mildred looked down upon her aunt curled comfortably asleep, oblivious to her surroundings, she wondered if Mrs. Pepperman was still picking at her olives or if she'd gotten herself mixed up somewhere. Mildred had a mind to find out.

Marley had disappeared. Mildred pushed her way through the foyer and back into the drawing room, frantically scanning the area for any familiar faces. There was Mrs. Pepperman, talking to the wallpaper, her plate empty. Morgan was standing where she and Marley had left her. Nick was at her side with his hands stuffed in his pockets, and standing right in front of them was—

"Adrian Belmont-Telfair will stop at nothing to harass my family. We should have kept him under our scrutiny."

Marley had materialized beside Mildred.

"I don't think he's harassing anyone," Mildred commented, but she kept a steady eye on the foppish fiend. He *was* standing—*leaning*—a little too close to Morgan. There was a certain wickedness in his countenance that Mildred couldn't quite name, but she could see Morgan squirming under its clutch.

"You're right," Mildred asserted. "I don't like him being here at all."

Marley marched towards Adrian. Mildred stuck to his side, pulling herself up as tall as she could. Marley leapt right up to Adrian in time to slap Adrian's roving hand away from Morgan's arm.

"What do you think you're doing?" Marley snapped. "Keep your waxy fingers away from my sister."

Mildred side-stepped out of the way. Adrian careened toward Marley until the two of them were fairly nose-to-nose.

"It'd be wise of you, Mortale, to first follow your own advice," Adrian sneered, shaking with disgust the hand that Marley had smacked.

Everyone in their immediate surroundings had gone a bit quiet, and the politer ones tried not to stare. The band kept playing, not paying any mind to the conundrum occurring just feet away.

"Don't assume for a moment that I'd ever pursue your sister, anyhow," Adrian continued. "If she's anything like your mother, she's a pitiful disaster."

Murmuring ensued. Fans were drawn.

"What, you have nothing to say?" Adrian smirked. "That's unusual. You're not as clever as I thought you were, after all. Though it makes sense, being raised by a father who can't keep—"

Quick as a flash camera, Marley drew back a fist and punched Adrian in his impeccable nose. Adrian reeled backward, saved from the floor by Morgan and Nick, who caught him and put him upright where he stood, dazed and bloodied.

The music paused after one last resonating, banjo pluck. The small audience that had gathered whispered furiously amongst themselves.

Adrian scrambled away from Morgan and Nick, lifting an arm to his wounded nose. His eyes glistened with tears as he sniffed back gushing blood.

"Look now what you've done," he whined into his tailored jacket's sleeve. "This is *gabardine.*"

Some of the witnesses to the whole ordeal snickered. The band, after a quick exchange of unwary glances, vaulted back into the song they'd left unfinished.

"Shut up, all of you! *Shut up!*" screeched Adrian.

"MARLEY!" Mother came bustling through. Father bumbled right at her heels. Mr. and Mrs. Belmont-Telfair rushed to Adrian's comfort as Mother ran to Marley.

"Marley, what were you thinking?!" Mother cried, glancing over at Adrian, whose own mother was delicately wiping away blood from his face with a lace handkerchief while his father frowned down at him.

"Please accept an apology from me on behalf of my son's behavior," Mother implored Mr. and Mrs. Belmont-Telfair. "I am mortified."

"No, we're the ones who should be apologizing," Mr. Belmont-Telfair said. "Really. I know how *impetuous* Adrian can be."

Adrian gaped. "Father!"

"Be quiet, Adrian," Mr. Belmont-Telfair quipped. "You embarrass me. Yes, the Mortale boy is a little strange, but you were antagonizing him."

Adrian sank into his mother's clutch. She kissed him on the head and clasped him to her slim frame.

"Thank you for your hospitality tonight, Maria," Mr. Belmont-Telfair nodded to Mother. "But we really must leave. We've had a most...interesting time."

"Thank you for coming," Mother replied in a shocked monotone.

Mr. Belmont-Telfair nodded to Mother and Father before he swept out of the room, trailed closely by Mrs. Belmont-Telfair, who guided away the still-sniffling Adrian.

After they'd walked a considerable distance away, Father exhaled and leaned into Marley. "That was thoroughly unexpected. Nicely done."

Marley smiled and nodded, shaking the bony hand he'd used to assault Adrian. "The horrible creature is gone at last."

A series of horrified shouts erupted from the dining room.

"Oh, what can be happening, now?" bemoaned Mother.

Mildred ran toward the commotion. A group of guests had crowded around the table, staring in stunned terror at the tabletop, which appeared to be *wriggling.*

The closer Mildred inched toward the sprawling mess on the table, the more clearly she recognized individual bodies of small black and brown creatures—with their spindly little legs, their multitude of unblinking eyes, and lightly furred bodies. They crept all over the peach cobbler, the finger sandwiches, and into the punch bowl.

Mother yelped from behind Mildred. "I told you to check the house for spiders!"

Mildred hadn't a moment to think up or utter a defense. A lady who stood nearby—the woman who had claimed to be Mother's oldest friend—clutched her heart and cried, "Is your home *usually* infested with spiders?"

Mother shook her head frantically. "No! No, of course not."

"Where are they *coming* from?" Morgan choked out.

She and Nick had mazed themselves to the forefront of the scene. Mildred's attention was pulled briefly to her sister's hand buried deep in the crook of Nick's arm.

"Let me see."

Marley slipped past Mildred, excitedly scanning the frenzied, scurrying creatures. He cupped one in his hands and craned his neck towards it. It walked warily across his palms.

"It seems like nothing more than a *Filistata hibernalis*," he said. "The common house spider. She's a bit large for her species, but harmless the same."

He let the spider walk off his hand and back onto the table.

"You *idiot!*" Morgan huffed. "Don't put it back where it came from! Kill it!"

Marley was indignant. "Spiders kill pests in the home. Do you want our house to be ridden with earwigs and cockroaches?"

The spiders spilled off the table and dropped to the floor, scurrying confusedly around people's shoes and skirts, and hurrying up the walls.

Pandemonium sprung loose.

"Get away! Get away!" one woman screeched, scrambling atop a chair, hopelessly poking her fan at the quickly advancing spiders.

"My new Chippendale!" gasped Mother.

"Good idea!" shouted another lady, hurtling herself atop Mother's writing desk. "The furniture is a refuge!"

"No, it's not!" Mother protested. "It's a horrible idea! Get down!"

"Listen, everyone, getting on top of furniture won't work," Marley cried. "They can climb. You have to scoop them up— like this."

He demonstrated, bending down and grabbing two generous handfuls of spiders.

This did not ease the panic.

The band barreled into a folksy quadrille, but no one found any partners because they were fleeing the room.

Mildred sank to the rug and gathered as many spiders as she could, even though she hadn't an idea of what she was going to do with them. The more she captured, the harder it became to keep them from escaping.

To her relief, Marley produced an enormous pot—taken from the sink of dirty dishes from tonight, judging by the saucy stains inside ("better to trap the spiders with" he said)—and he, Mildred, Morgan, and Nick began the task of dumping the animals into the pot. Mildred stared into the dark, writhing mass as she released handful after handful into the receptacle. A sickening scratching noise emanated from inside the pot as dozens of the creatures, tangled in each other, attempted to climb up the slick sides of their metal prison.

It seemed to Mildred that the stream of arachnids was never-ending—but as mysteriously as they had all appeared, they simply stopped arriving. Marley and Nick hoisted the pot off the floor and hastily pushed through the crowd toward the back door to dispose of its contents.

In the drawing room, the band chorused lyrics to a popular song, No one sang along.

Mr. and Mrs. Upchurch had made their way to the door and were hurriedly gathering their things, talking to each in hushed tones. Mother dashed over.

Mrs. Upchurch's face flushed as she struggled to pin her hat on, giving Mother a strained smile. "Oh, Maria. I apologize, we were hoping to leave without any fuss."

"That was just an anomaly," Mother insisted. "It's all taken care of now."

Mrs. Upchurch laid a gloved hand on Mother's arm. She leaned in, lowering her voice. "Really, Maria. We're doing you a favor. We cannot stay here any longer and allow you to embarrass yourself. Good night."

After a few patronizing pats on Mother's arm, Mrs. Upchurch turned and walked out.

"Thank you for your efforts." Mr. Upchurch tilted his hat to Mother, then followed his wife.

Mother slammed the door shut in his wake.

A sudden, unexplainable chill set into Mildred then. She glimpsed a white-grey haze pass by her, and her breath caught in her chest. As if someone had swung open the door on a windy night, a gust swept through the rooms, carrying away the light—the hall sconces, the gas lamps, the chandeliers on every ceiling—with it in one fell swoop.

The band fell silent, finally. A low murmuring filled the air like the hum of summer cicadas.

The dishes on the dining room table began to rattle. The furniture shook. Ladies' fans were torn out of their hands and catapulted across the room by unseen forces. Glasses of punch shattered in guests' hands, splattering liquid onto the floor, the walls, the furniture, and faces.

All propriety lost, ladies and gentlemen of the highest esteem dashed for the front door in screaming droves, dodging flying vases, floating finger foods, and other frantic partygoers.

Marley and Nick walked into the foyer to witness the disorder in full swing. As they stood speechless and immobile, an empty glass was pitched toward Marley's head. He bowed out of the way, and it struck Uncle Edmund, who had been searching for Aunt Ola in the fray.

"Excuse me, ma'am."

Mother turned to see the band shuffling awkwardly before her. The fiddler and the banjoist clutched their instruments like shields, while the boy gripped his spoons aloft, waving them about defensively.

"Yes?" Mother asked rather brusquely, brushing away some flyaway hairs that had stuck to her face.

"I think we better leave, now," the fiddler said. "I think you understand why." She blocked a rogue statuette with her instrument.

"Yes, yes, go." Mother shooed them toward the door.

"Thank you!" shouted the banjoist, as the three of them fled the house. "It was a lotta fun!"

"Well, *I* was having a nice time," Mrs. Pepperman said as she hobbled out the door with the musicians, raising her glass to Mother.

No one protested that she had left with one of the family's last remaining crystal glasses.

THE LIGHTS FLICKERED back on after all the guests had left. The last one to leave was Nick, awkward and silent, who gave Morgan a handshake goodnight and told her, Mildred, and Marley to visit him in the cemetery sometime.

The house was devastated. As she went about picking up shards of glass and bits of broken chairs, Mother sobbed, wailing on about what a disappointment everyone and everything was. Eventually, she gave up, announcing that she was going to bed. Father retreated wordlessly to his study, leaving Mildred, Marley, and Morgan alone with the vast mess at hand.

None of them knew how to fix the chaos, so none of them attempted to.

Aunt Camella staggered awake, studying her surroundings in oblivious wonder. "Where did the orphans go? My, but it's quiet in here, isn't it?"

They had, until this moment, forgotten about Aunt Camella completely. Somehow, the woman had indulged in enough punch to knock her senseless during the worst parts of the evening.

"Well, if we're all just going to stand here and do nothing, I'm leaving," Marley said. With a nod, he ran to the stairs, hopping them two at a time.

Aunt Camella let out a breath and shook her head. "I feel *very* sleepy."

Mildred and Morgan assisted Aunt Camella upstairs, which took much longer than it should have because she kept pausing to throw her head back in laughter.

"What a night!" she roared. "Such fun."

"Indeed," agreed Mildred.

CHAPTER THIRTEEN

WHEN MILDRED AWOKE it was half-past noon. Aunt
Camella's bed was rumpled and abandoned. Muffled discord
rose from downstairs.

She quickly dressed and then tore down the stairs and into
the foyer, a stocking slipping down her leg and her hair, half-
heartedly brushed, flying into her face as she skipped over an
array of personal belongings (a fan, a few watches, a string of
pearls) left behind from the panic the previous night. All
around, furniture was strewn and upset, and punch stained the
hardwood and the carpet and the walls, appearing ominously
like dried blood.

Hesitantly, Mildred followed the disturbance into the dining
room. At the table, Mother wept into her hands. Aunt Camella
sat beside her, patting Mother's shoulder in awkward
consolation. Marley was slumped over the tabletop and Morgan
glared down at him. Father anxiously paced the floor behind
them all.

Mildred took a seat quietly as she could, feeling as if she were disturbing a scene in a play. Aunt Camella gave her a small, sad, close-lipped smile.

"Sit, sit," Father murmured, continuing his nervous patrol.

"So, what's wrong?" Mildred asked.

Mother sniffled, brought her hands away from her face, and sighed. She wiped at her face with the heels of her hands and then lifted a paper that was lying on the table in front of her. She shook it at Mildred, falling back into tears.

Mildred leaned over the table to read—

TO THE PUBLIC.

I challenge Marley Mortale it a public duel at three o'clock in the afternoon at Wright Square. Mr. Mortale, in an OUTRAGEOUS and COWARDLY manner, assaulted my character last night during a social gathering. The duel will be to maim, and pistols the weapon of choice.

I announce Marley Mortale to be LOW-CLASS & A POLTROON, and notify the city accordingly.

"How ridiculous," concluded Mildred.

"I know, dueling has been out of style for years," Marley grumbled. "Also, how did they manage to get so many printed so quickly?"

"What do you mean? How many of them are there?"

"They're posted all over the city." Aunt Camella shook her head. "This one was delivered right to our door by the Belmont-Telfair's butler."

"Can't Marley...not do it?" Mildred suggested.

"Unthinkable!" Marley exclaimed. "I'm going to give that sneaky muck snipe what for."

"Well, at least it's only to maim," Mildred noted.

She thought that would help ease the unrest. Instead, everyone raised their opinions, their simultaneous responses to Mildred's comment mixing in a screeching cacophony. Father paced faster, all the while spitting profanities about the Belmont-Telfairs. Marley began a shouting match with Morgan, and Aunt Camella struggled between trying to comfort Mother and trying to calm them both.

Mildred stood witness to this mess, her head swimming.

"Okay, okay, *okay!*" Father shouted.

The room quieted.

Father's hands were clamped on either side of his head, which he shook back and forth as if rattling out a nightmare. His glasses wobbled and then settled crookedly on his nose. He shut his eyes and exhaled.

"Okay. I'm trying to remember...I read once about this sort of thing. I've never been challenged myself, of course...not the type..."

"Get on with it, already!" Aunt Camella huffed.

Father's eyes popped open. "Camella do be quiet. Now, as is customary, each contender needs a second, usually a trusted friend who aids them before and during the event, helping to select his weapon and be a mediator between the two—"

"I want Mildred to be my second," Marley declared with a decisive nod. He leaned back and crossed his arms.

Father blinked. "A thirteen-year-old girl cannot be your second, Marley."

"I'm thirteen and a *half*," Mildred protested.

Father, not any more convinced, crossed his arms and shook his head.

Marley shrugged. "It's my choice. And I choose Mildred."

"I want to do it," Mildred blurted. "I mean, I *can* do it. If I'm allowed."

Father let out a sigh and rubbed his forehead. "I suppose if that's what Marley wishes...although I've never heard of such a thing..."

Mother burst into another bout of tears. "Oh! This whole day is a mess."

"It's only one o'clock," Marley commented.

"*Don't you speak!*" Mother shouted, shaking with anger.

"Ah, well," Aunt Camella sighed. She stood. "I'll go put on my outdoor clothes. You know, I woke up today feeling a little woozy. I wonder if it was something I ate last night? I can hardly remember..."

"IT'S A VERY NICE VIEW." Aunt Camella sat beside Mildred on the blanket she'd brought along to the designated dueling site. She's spread the quilt on the center of the grassy expanse facing the William Washington Gordon Monument. The towering pedestal overlooked the cobblestoned path where Marley and his adversary were to perform their "silly little squabble" as Morgan had so affectionately referred to it on their walk over.

Aunt Camella shifted, reached into the recesses of her skirt, and procured a pair of brass opera glasses. She squinted into them, even though there wasn't much to look at presently.

Mildred recognized the object from an evening long ago, when the family went to see a special performance of a Jenny Lind impersonator. "Aren't those Marley's?"

"Indeed, they are," Aunt Camella answered. She dangled them in Mildred's face. "Wouldn't you like to see?"

Mildred gently nudged Aunt Camella's hand away. Mother stood nearby with hands clasped tightly, appearing to be on the verge of weeping. Morgan, standing next to her, looked as neutral as ever. Marley, arms folded tightly, paced up and down the path, while Father, his head hung low, treaded harried circles. Together they looked like a pair of madmen.

A small crowd had already gathered, ladies with their fans and gossip on their tongues, men with serious faces and scrutinizing eyes. Mildred hugged her knees, tucked some hair behind her ear, scratched her nose, sighed, and tucked some hair behind her other ear.

Aunt Camella whacked her with the opera glasses.

"Ah!" Mildred cried, rubbing her arm. "What was that for?"

"Stop it with all that fidgeting," Aunt Camella said. "You're not helping yourself." She glanced about and then leaned in closer, speaking low. "And if I were you, I'd cover up those legs. You're in public."

Mildred glanced upon her black-stockinged legs. "I'm wearing stockings."

Aunt Camella sighed and shook her head. "This generation with their 'stockings'. When I was your age, if a girl showed her legs off like that she could get kicked out."

"Of where?"

"The state!" Aunt Camella cried. "Goodness...oh, look! Adrian's arrived!"

Mildred's heart palpitated and she shakily got to her feet. She felt the burn of curious stares on her back as she approached Father and Marley.

"What are *you* doing?" Adrian snarled at Mildred as he pulled on a pair of gloves. "This is no place for a girl."

"I'm Marley's second," Mildred proudly answered.

Adrian threw his head back and laughed, but Mildred stood her ground. She fixed on Adrian what she imagined was a strong stare. She willed herself not to blink, even when she felt her eyeballs twitch from the heat. A solemnity seemed to befall Adrian, and he shifted uncomfortably.

"Let's get this over with," Marley grumbled.

He'd marched to Mildred, hooked an arm through Mildred's, and pulled her along. Father walked with them wordlessly, and when they reached a reasonable distance away from the enemy, he took both by the shoulder and turned them to face him. His face was stern as his eyes darted between the two of them.

"There is quite a lot at stake right now," he said. "Mildred, before this goes any further, I want you to talk to Adrian. See if you can come to some sort of...last-minute compromise."

Mildred's throat tightened. "Um, okay. I'll try."

Marley gave her a nod and then shoved her forward in Adrian's direction. She tripped and stumbled to her knees, scraping her knee on the cobblestoned ground, but sprung to her feet in a flash. Her stocking had torn a little. She could feel the humidity on her exposed, raw skin as she tramped ahead.

"I suppose you've come to me with a request for mercy," Adrian remarked when Mildred had come close enough.

"If that's what you want to call it," Mildred replied. "Adrian, must we continue with this?"

"I'm quite sure," he snapped, his snarl dropping into a frown. "And don't you *dare* try to challenge me."

"You're being dramatic," said Mildred.

Adrian's hand shook as he lifted a finger to Mildred's face. "I've had enough of you and your brother. I might have considered calling it off, but you've just solidified my decision."

Mildred rolled her eyes. "Okay, *fine.*"

Then she went back running to Marley and Father.

"He's even more annoyed, isn't he?" Marley said.

"It seems so," Mildred responded, a little out of breath.

"That was an earnest attempt, Mildred," Father said. "Now..." He lifted the lid of the oak box he'd carried with him, exposing an ivory-handled pistol nestled in a bed of red velvet.

"This was my grandfather's. *I've* never used it, though it is a beautiful thing, isn't it? It's troubling to think that a work of craftsmanship such as this can be used to inflict so much pain and tragedy..."

Marley's fingers danced over the weapon and snatched it out of its home. He tugged Mildred's arm outwards, pinched open her hand, and slapped the instrument on her open palm.

"Alright, Millie," he sighed, placing a hand on her shoulder. "Hand me my weapon."

Mildred returned the pistol to Marley.

"Thanks, little sister," he said.

"Okay," Mildred said, and she ran back to Aunt Camella's blanket.

Mildred looked over to Adrian. His family servant finished polishing his Flintlock and handed it to Adrian, who accepted it graciously. Mr. Belmont-Telfair stepped forward. The people gathered around quieted.

"Gentlemen," he said. "Shake hands."

Marley stepped right up to Adrian and stuck out his hand. After a moment's hesitation, Adrian grasped it, gave it one feeble shake, and then dropped it. Marley nodded and then turned away.

"Now, wait a minute, Marley," Mr. Belmont-Telfair started, "You must both follow proper procedure..."

Marley, rolling his eyes, made a show of turning around and walking back to his starting point.

"Oh, Lord," Mother sighed. She buried her face in her hands.

"Marley, Adrian, it is my obligation to remind you that this battle is *only to maim*," Mr. Belmont-Telfair announced. "Any move taken deliberately to injure your opponent fatally is against regulations and will result in lawful action. Now, in ten seconds, at my count, you will both turn and take ten paces."

Mr. Belmont-Telfair began to count. Mother, her face still covered, turned her head aside. Mrs. Belmont-Telfair watched her son with glistening eyes and clasped hands, although she wore a prideful little smile.

The countdown reached its end, and Marley and Adrian turned to face each other. Adrian was shaking; Mildred could see his trembling from yards away. Marley stood perfectly collected, which made Mildred smile.

"Ready your weapons," Mr. Belmont-Telfair shouted.

Steadily, Marley raised Father's pistol with the demeanor of a seasoned soldier. Adrian's stance was decidedly less impressive. He brought his other hand to the handle of the gun to steady his grip.

Aunt Camella, rapt, brought out the opera glasses again, which elicited a scoff from Mother.

"Camella, what are you doing? We're not at the races."

Aunt Camella waved away Mother's disdain. "Things are getting serious now."

"Shoot in one," Mr. Belmont-Telfair began.

Marley was unmoving as a statue. Adrian narrowed his eyes. "Two."

Adrian took a moment to brush some hair away from his face. His coiffed locks had turned stringy.

"Three."

Marley readied his pistol and had nearly pulled the trigger when, with a shriek, Adrian flung his family heirloom weapon to the ground. The crowd murmured restlessly.

Adrian cowered to the cobblestone.

"Please!" He cried. "Don't do it! I surrender! Don't do it!"

Marley lowered his arm, looking serious for a moment. Then he whirled around, tossed the pistol in Mildred's general direction (she just barely caught it), and then broke into a triumphant grin.

"HA!" He exclaimed. "Who's a low-class poltroon *now*?"

"What does that word mean, exactly?" Aunt Camella wondered aloud.

No one replied. They were staring in disbelief at Adrian, still on the ground, who was now weeping. He grabbed a nearby stone and hurled it with a frustrated cry. Marley watched it skitter across the cobblestone to his feet. Mrs. Belmont-Telfair rushed to Adrian and stooped to his level, smothering him in hugs and kisses.

Aunt Camella whistled. "My, what a show. That was great."

Mother ran to Marley. Before he had a moment to escape, she'd wrapped him up in her arms and was sobbing into his shoulder. He reluctantly endured the public display of affection.

Mother let him go, dried her tears with her glove, and smiled. "I'm just so happy you're not hurt. I was so scared for you."

Marley straightened and adjusted his collar. "I would've won, anyhow."

"Are you so sure of that?" Morgan quipped as she sauntered over.

"Marley!" Nick blundered over, seemingly from out of the bushes. He took Marley by the shoulders and shook him. "I can't believe it. What a turn of events. Adrian finally broke down, that good-for-nothing scoundrel!"

Marley beamed. "Spoken like an honest friend."

"I didn't know you had a friend, Marley," Mother said. She turned to Nick. "Who are you?"

"Nick Dobson."

"Of the ship merchants Dobson?"

"Yes, ma'am."

Mother nodded, evidently impressed by Marley's social connections. "Well now, I suppose we should leave for home before anything else...interesting happens."

Mildred lagged behind the rest of her family. She glanced behind her as the crowd dispersed, confused and a little disappointed. Adrian stood with his head hung low, while his mother rubbed his shoulders and his father towered over him, shouting. Mildred couldn't make out what he was saying, but to her shock, she felt something like pity for Adrian. She had a feeling that Marley wasn't about to be bothered by him for a little while.

"Come on, Millie!" Marley shouted to her. "We're losing you up here."

Mildred ran to his side and didn't look back again.

BY THE TIME they had reached home, the family's bewildered murmurings over Marley's victory had subsided. Mildred once again found herself lingering a few feet behind everyone else, lost in her thoughts. Therefore, she was not the first one to enter the house—but she certainly heard Mother's horrified scream.

The downstairs, which remained in disarray from the party, had been further ravaged and bizarrely rearranged. The chandelier in the dining room dangled precariously from a gap in the ceiling. The dining room table was set diagonally on its side, and the chairs had been stacked atop one another in the center of the room. The piano was missing; Morgan discovered it halfway shoved into one of the downstairs closets. The paintings—which Mother had so carefully chosen from a local gallery, promised by the seller to be invaluable—were slashed down the middle of their rustic sceneries and refined still lifes. Over the fireplace, the family portrait was upside down.

Marley dashed to the basement, fearing for whatever he kept down there.

Mother was in despair. She spent the rest of the afternoon and all evening shuffling around the house, sniffing back tears and filling the air with sighs while everyone else worked to set things back to normal. Every time Mother entered Mildred's vicinity with her anxious, watery face, Mildred grew self-conscious of her terrible knowledge.

That night, as Mildred listened to Aunt Camella's soft snores and held Mortem close to her chest, she made a silent promise to herself to put an end to all of this before it carried on much longer. Before she could think up a decent solution, she fell into a slumber, the muffled noises of moving furniture scraping across the floor below.

CHAPTER FOURTEEN

IT WAS MID-AUGUST, a relentless stretch of sweltering summer that reminded everyone that the relief of early autumn was still long out of reach. Mildred sat at the bottom of the staircase, an untouched book shut on her lap, observing the afternoon mundanity.

Mother hurried through the foyer, oblivious to Mildred. She trailed sweet perfume (vanilla and something like sugared violet, Mildred thought, a change from her usual sharp musk) in her march toward the parlor. Mildred heard her shuffling around the wilting floral arrangements, her shoes crushing the dried petals on the hardwood.

In the drawing room, Aunt Camella murmured to herself; in her mind's eye, Mildred saw her aunt occupied with her usual routine: stitching linens while cutting coupons from the local newspaper. ("Five cents off a facial toner, Mildred," she'd touted just yesterday. "Staying inside has not done your complexion any favors.")

Marley stepped out from the basement, sending Mildred a sympathetic stare. He shut the door and padded to the stairs, patting Mildred on the shoulder on his way up.

Mortem hopped onto Mildred's lap, carelessly knocking away the book. It skittered across the foyer floor. Mildred made no move to retrieve it.

He snuggled against her, purring and looking up at her with large, round eyes. Mildred hugged him close to her chest, burying her face in his fur as she tried to shut her mind to unpleasantries.

Time had passed so strangely.

IT HAD BEEN three weeks since The Incident on the day of Marley's victory against Adrian. Hence, every day, the family had awoken to similarly strange occurrences, from slightly rearranged furniture to windows, doors, and cabinets spontaneously opening and shutting to missing items (the potato peelers couldn't be found for two weeks, which was especially upsetting to Aunt Camella, who had to put a moratorium on the baking of her funeral potatoes. Marley finally located the instruments stacked in a corner in the basement).

None of these events were distressing enough to invoke anything but near-constant irritation, which was always felt and never addressed.

In that first week, Mildred decided that it was time for her to wrangle her siblings for another intervention regarding the thing that still loomed in their collective consciousness. Following a somber, hushed dinner (family gatherings had been increasingly so; even Aunt Camella had keyed down), they all ducked into the hallway closet.

"Alright," Marley sighed, crossing his arms. "What is it, now?"

"You know very well why we're here," Mildred hissed. "It's the same thing it's been all summer."

"Oh, you mean Mother's little thefts," Marley grumbled. "Sorry to tell you, Mildred, but *you're* the one who insisted on turning this into a whole ordeal."

"What do you mean?" Mildred's throat was tight.

"I helped you get the 'proof' you needed, Millie. I don't know what else you want me to do. You're on your own with this, now."

"That's not fair, Marley," Morgan interjected. "None of this is Mildred's fault."

"That might be true, but she didn't have to drag us into it, either," snapped Marley.

"I'm sorry that you feel the way you do, Marley, but you've known the same things I've known for almost just as long, and you wouldn't have done a thing about it if I hadn't insisted," Mildred asserted.

"And why should I have?" Marley asked. "To be honest, I don't care what Mother does or doesn't do. None of this affects me—or you, for that matter. You'd be better off just to move on."

"Marley!" gasped Morgan.

"Save me your scorn." Marley rolled his eyes.

"The responsibility to fix this situation can't be just mine," Mildred stressed.

"Sure, it can," Marley said. "You're the one who...summoned all of this."

"What do you mean?" Mildred felt her face growing hot.

"All I'm saying is that *you're* the one who can see them, the ghosts—or whatever they are," Marley said. "All of this started getting worse that night we returned from the cemetery, which, as I recall, was a trip we made due to your paranoia."

"*Paranoia?*" Angry tears smarted in Mildred's eyes, blurring Marley's scowl. "I was right!"

"Who's to say that the whole confrontation with Lucia wouldn't have happened anyway, regardless of what we did that night?" Morgan suggested. "Not to mention that it was your suggestion, Marley, that we go to the cemetery."

"Okay, so now both Mildred and I have some blame in this mess. Where does that leave you?" Marley challenged.

"Oh, just *stop!*" Mildred cried, beating Marley with alternating fists and open palms.

Morgan grabbed her from behind and jerked her away from Marley, who'd barely flinched under the attack.

"Calm down, Mildred," Morgan chastised. She shook her head. "I'm surprised at you."

Mildred felt flushed. The air in the tiny space had suddenly become a little too dense. She picked at her collar and patted down some loose strings of hair, which had curled in the heat. She inhaled through her shortening breath.

"I'm sorry," she said, trying to keep her voice level despite the upset that was blanketing her. "I'm scared, and I'm tired, and I'm frustrated. I don't like knowing what I do, and I don't like how long I've gone knowing it without doing something about it. I feel like everyone expects something from me."

"Oh, Millie," Morgan sighed. She hugged Mildred to her side.

Marley lifted his head and looked to Mildred, although he still bore a frown. "I guess I'm a little sorry, too."

"All of this arguing is making us ignore the real culprit," Mildred sniffed. "Mother is the one who is committing the crimes here, not any of us."

This turned everyone silent for a few moments.

Mildred lifted her head. "I'll say something about it."

"When?" asked Morgan.

"I don't know," Mildred admitted. "But I will. I have to. I'll think over how I'm going to approach the whole thing, of course. I want to wait for a good time when we're all together, the whole family." Mildred's confidence waned as she imagined the scenario. She nodded slowly. "I can do it. Not today, maybe not soon, but I can do it."

Marley clapped his hands together. Mildred and Morgan flinched. "That's the spirit. Now, if you don't mind, I'm leaving this horrible space. It's smaller than a family mausoleum in here."

He nodded to his sisters and then escaped. Morgan let go of Mildred and kissed her on the forehead. "It'll be all right, Millie...well, someday it will be, at least."

"How do you know?" Mildred asked.

"I don't *know*," Morgan replied, her eyes lingering on Mildred's for a few moments. "But I hope."

Mildred was grateful that Marley wasn't around to make a statement about how hope was just a flimsy mental construct.

Morgan slipped out of the closet and gently pushed the door shut behind her, but the door creaked back open just a little so a tiny sliver of light from the hallway flooded into the room. Mildred remained in the tiny room, staring into the weak light from the single bulb, relishing the quietness of being alone.

Suddenly a shadow passed over the light; Mildred quickly tugged off the light and then froze. For a moment everything was still, and then the door opened, and Aunt Camella poked her head through.

"Mildred, what are you doing, you silly girl?" she asked with a smile.

Mildred shifted a bit and averted eye contact. "I was looking for something."

"Did you find it?"

"Not really," Mildred replied.

Aunt Camella's head swiveled to and fro, surveying the closet. "Well, it's no wonder you didn't. It's black as night in here!"

"Oh, yeah," Mildred said lamely. "I guess so. Thanks, Aunt Camella. I'll look for it later."

Mildred forced herself to smile and stepped into the foyer, scooted past her aunt, and then made a dash for the stairs.

A FEW DAYS passed without much activity at all. Everyone practically tip-toed about the house, anticipating something weird or unexpected, that they would walk into a room that had been turned upside down, or be overcome by a sudden cold spell. Mildred, Marley, and Morgan hardly spoke to one another, going through their routines encapsulated in their own concerns. But every time the three of them were together, both Marley and Morgan shot Mildred questioning looks, while Mildred avoided looking at anyone.

Mother, who noticed these exchanges, was annoyed.

"What is the matter with all of you?" she huffed.

"Oh," Aunt Camella started, "I didn't know—"

"Not *you*, Camella—them!" Mother gestured towards Mildred, Marley, and Morgan. "The purpose of having meals together as a family is to speak to one another."

"When did we ever do that?" Marley laughed.

"Oh, everyone is together? I don't see Father here," Morgan grumbled, stabbing a bit of potato with her fork.

"Oh!" Mother cried out. She stood and pushed her chair aside. "I've had enough."

She bustled away.

"Gracious," said Aunt Camella. "Well, I was enjoying the silence. Conversations turn too quickly into nonsense in this house."

That night, as Mildred struggled to fall asleep, she saw a silvery glow darting past her periphery. She sat up immediately, scanning the room. Aunt Camella was softly asleep, turned on her side away from Mildred's view. Mortem lifted his head, his ears perked. Mildred looked all around and above her, and when she looked away from the ceiling she came face-to-face with a glowering Lucia.

"*Ah!*" Mildred flinched.

She peeked over to the bed. Aunt Camella remained quietly at rest, her body rising gently with breath. Mildred turned back to Lucia. Her specter cousin's torso protruded from the middle of the cot, her arms splayed out.

"You frightened me, Lucia," Mildred hissed.

Lucia scoffed. She rolled her eyes as the rest of her rose into view, and she gracefully glided into a supine pose at Mildred's feet. "Of course, I frightened you. It's the only way to get your attention."

Mildred shifted into a more upright position to better see Lucia. "No, it's not. You *can* just appear to me in a non-intrusive, somewhat pleasant way."

Mortem walked onto Mildred's lap and nestled there, keeping a watchful glare on Lucia.

"Oh, stop looking at me like that," Lucia sighed. Mildred wasn't sure if she was referring to Mortem, or herself. Lucia turned her head to face Mildred. "You know, I *am* sorry."

"What about?"

"I don't know." Lucia faced the ceiling again. "I mean...what I guess I mean to say is that I sort of regret not being friendlier to you when I was...not the way I am now."

"Why are you saying all this?" Mildred couldn't *not* be suspicious of Lucia's intentions. She waited for an answer. The only sound in the room was Aunt Camella's soft snores. "Lucia, what do you want?"

Lucia's response was to burst into wailing.

"*Shhh!*" Mildred cried in a whisper. *"What is the matter?"*

"Oh, no one can hear me but you, anyway." Lucia sniffled and wiped her tears away. "Oh, Mildred. Please don't be cross with me."

Mildred sat very still, her heart hammering.

"Don't tell Aunt Mar—your mother," Lucia begged. She leapt across the cot and clasped Mildred's hand in an icy grip that sent a shiver up Mildred's arm. "Please, I beg of you. Don't tell her you know what she's done."

"What?" Mildred was shocked. "Lucia, this is absurd. I made a promise to Marley and Morgan—I made a promise to *myself*. I thought you *wanted* me to say something."

"I know," Lucia sighed woefully, blinking her big eyes. "I was, at first...I thought it would make me feel better about my predicament, and I thought if you confronted your mother about it and she changed her ways then everything would be resolved. But I've changed my mind about the whole thing."

"Why?" Mildred tried to tug her hand away from Lucia's, but Lucia's hold was solid as stone. Mildred used her other hand to pry her hand free. "What about the other...you know, the others like you? You're not the only one affected by all of this."

"They don't have to know." Lucia shook her head.

"They get to know things, one way or another, anyhow," Mildred said. "I imagine you understand that better than me."

"You're right, you *don't* understand!" Lucia snapped. She flew away from the cot, turning her back to Mildred.

"I don't, because you're explaining anything!" Mildred protested.

Lucia lowered herself to the edge of the cot. "I don't want to go."

"What do you mean?"

Lucia stared blankly ahead. "If you confront your mother, and the truth is out, and everything is solved, all of us—me and the others—are going to leave. But I don't want to leave. I'm scared. I like it here. This is the only place I've ever been. How can I just...*go* somewhere else, forever? I don't know anything except for this."

"But you can't stay here forever," Mildred said, softly.

"How do *you* know?" Lucia's accusatory tone returned. "You don't know anything. You're not sick, and you have a family, and you have a *future*. I don't have any of those things anymore."

"I hardly see my father," Mildred began, her voice trembling. "My mother is having a nervous breakdown. Morgan hasn't been happy all summer. Marley is impulsive and arrogant and I'm—"

"I don't want to hear about any of your problems!" Lucia clamped her hands over her ears, her eyes shut tightly. "Stop it, *stop* it!"

"You're being selfish," Mildred spat. "All you care about is your comfort. But you're not the only lost soul who's suffering—

not in this house, and not in this world. I'm sick of trying to solve other people's problems, and I'm certainly not going to solve yours. I know what I'm going to do, and I'm going to stick to it. You're never going to stop me."

Lucia's expression had hardened into a spiteful scowl the likes of which Mildred had never seen.

"Oh, Mildred..." Lucia shook her head. "You've made the wrong decision. Good night, cousin. I hope you don't have any nightmares."

She faded into the air, leaving a chill in her wake. Mildred scooped Mortem close to her. He tried to squiggle out of her clutches, but she held him tight and buried her face in his fur. After she felt reasonably calm, she let him go. He jumped to the floor, shaking himself off.

Mildred frowned down at him. He stretched, yawned, and then trotted away.

Feeling cold and lonely, Mildred curled onto her side and finally slipped into an exhausted slumber.

MILDRED JOLTED AWAKE to a thunderous crash from below. A moment of pause was followed by an explosion of sparring voices.

She got out of bed, wobbly with fatigue. Aunt Camella had already woken, and her bed was made up neatly. Mildred quickly slipped out of her nightgown and into a housedress and then crept downstairs. She followed the spat to the dining room, where Marley was hunched over the floor, picking up pieces of a shattered vase from a pool of water and shattered ceramic.

"Marley threw a fit and broke my vase," Mother said. She stood over him, one hand pressed to her forehead, the other hugging her abdomen. "It was one of the last good ones I owned."

Marley paused his tidying. "No, I didn't. I accidentally bumped into the table where the vase was precariously balanced, and it fell."

Mother shook her head. "He came running in here, dashing from out of the basement like a madman, and immediately went right up to the first item he saw, *lifted* it—don't scowl and shake your head like that, Marley, I *saw* it—and *threw* it to the floor."

Mildred looked to Marley expectantly. He sighed and stood, fragments of broken vase cupped in both of his palms. "Lanthanum is sick."

Mildred gasped. "No!"

"Who in the world is Lanthanum?" Mother asked.

"She's my favorite mouse," Marley said.

"You did this because of a *mouse*?" Mother seethed.

Marley rolled his eyes. "Not just *one* mouse, Mother. A whole lot of them. About two-thirds, to be exact. And little Lanthanum is in the worst shape of all of them. Some of my other animals have taken ill as well. Valentino and Tallulah aren't going great, either. One of them's developed a terrible wheeze."

"What are Valentino and Tallulah?" Mother frowned.

"It doesn't matter, now." Marley waved away the question. "I've never had so many creatures of varying species fall ill at the same time—it's *suspicious*."

"Perhaps there is a contagious disease spreading amongst the animals," Mother suggested. "Something like yellow fever."

Marley scoffed. "Don't suggest anything unless you know what you're talking about, Mother."

"Don't you *dare* talk to me like that!" Mother snapped. She cast a shaking finger between Marley's eyes. "You've already caused enough grief for me today."

"What are you going to do about it?" Marley rebutted angrily, pushing aside Mother's finger. "I'm already trapped in this miserable old house with you, and I hardly ever get to do what I want. At this point, there's little you can take from me."

Mildred stepped a little closer to Marley. "Marley, no.

Stop—"

But he shifted away from her and carried on. "You can't threaten me, Mother. Nothing you can say will make me feel any remorse." He gazed at Mother with such intensity that she recoiled. "*I know things.*"

"What is *that* supposed to mean?" Mother choked, her eyes darting wildly.

Marley nodded to Mildred. "Go on, Millie. Say it."

Mildred shook her head as she backed away. "No. No."

"What is going on?" Mother's attention ricocheted between Marley's insistent stare and Mildred's reluctance.

"I'm sorry," Mildred said, her voice escaping barely a whisper. She turned and ran up the stairs, ignoring the two voices calling after her.

She was so bent on reaching her room that she collided with full force into Aunt Camella. It took a moment for Mildred to compose herself and realize what had happened as she stared blankly at her aunt, who wore an amused smile.

"Why, Mildred!" Aunt Camella chuckled. "You *have* been acting strangely lately! Hiding in closets, now running through the upstairs hallway...I must say, it's rather unlike you."

"Uh, yes," Mildred replied, looking everywhere except at Aunt Camella. "I, uh...I would like to go into my bedroom, if you don't mind."

Without waiting for an answer, she slipped past her aunt and into her room, shut the door, and proceeded to sit on the edge of her cot. She sighed and stared longingly at the bed, which she hadn't occupied in what seemed like a year, and where Mortem was currently curled up contentedly against a pillow. It was an unfamiliar one, square, with a motto ("Dulce Periculum") that looked decidedly hand stitched.

Mildred lay down on her cot and shut her eyes. She remained there for a long while, not sleeping, merely listening to the sounds of her breathing.

THE FOLLOWING WEEK was Marley's eighteenth birthday.

He hardly let a soul forget, even going so far as to tell grieving guests about the impending day, which did nothing to ease their pain. One lady burst into sobs, crying that her sister would have been twenty-three come September. Subsequently, Mother had taken Marley by the shoulders and promptly led him away to help set the table for the luncheon.

On that significant day, the weather was a pleasant eighty-five degrees, perfect for an outdoor celebration in the backyard. A small table had been set with plates, forks, and a neat little pile of presents.

Aunt Camella and Mother had worked together the evening before to bake a triple-layered cake, which they had burnt in their first attempt and had to begin again. The whole downstairs was smoky for hours.

Admittedly, the cake at hand also had a slightly unsettling, metallic taste, but for the sake of getting along, everyone soldiered on and ignored that little unpleasantry. Marley even helped himself to a second slice.

"Open your gifts, Marley," Mother urged.

Sucking icing off his thumb, Marley surveyed the collection of prettily wrapped boxes and packages. He grabbed a square box at the bottom of the heap. It was a nauseating shade of pink, tied with red ribbon.

"Oh, that one's from me." Aunt Camella smiled.

Marley ripped into the packaging. From out of layers of tissue paper, Marley lifted a pair of gilded goggles.

"Wonderful." He grinned, turning the item over in his hands. It sported a leather head strap and magnifying lenses.

Aunt Camella beamed. "They're hand-crafted, specially ordered. There's not another pair like that in the world. They match the gloves as well."

Eyes wide, Marley dug further into the gauzy paper and pulled out a pair of leather gloves. He rose them up to the sunlight to examine them and nodded in approval.

"Very nice," commented Father. (It was the only thing he said the entire evening.)

Mother glanced askance at Aunt Camella. her lips taut. Mildred knew she was displeased with Aunt Camella encouraging Marley's mysterious hobbies and habits but was relieved that nothing was said to spark an argument.

Marley tucked the goggles and gloves back in the wrapping and into the box, set it aside, and tore into another gift.

The rest of the evening continued comfortably. For the first time in a long while, there wasn't a single altercation or disagreement or insult amongst any of them. They all stayed outside until the sky began to grow dark, whence Mildred, Morgan, Mother, Father, and Aunt Camella carried the dishes and leftover cake inside while Marley gathered his gifts in his arms. Everyone in the household went to bed that night in decent moods.

And then the morning arrived.

Mildred gasped awake. It was early; the sky was barely light. The moment she'd woken, she'd known something was wrong. She'd felt it in the pit of her stomach, where she also felt an unpleasant stirring and ache. As she sat up, her arms limp and shaking, a rush of a headache throbbed dully in her temples. She glanced over at the bed. Aunt Camella was absent, but it wasn't made up nicely and neatly like it usually was. The duvet and pillows were crumpled, and it looked as if it had been vacated in a hurry.

A jolt of nausea ran through Mildred. She closed her eyes, trying to shut out the pain. A moment later, she lurched over the side of the cot and was emptied of last night's consumptions.

As she trembled, bent over in anguish, Mother and Aunt Camella rushed into the room. Both appeared unwell, their faces sallow, their eyes red and watery.

"Looks like she's sick, too," Mother sighed.

Aunt Camella sniffled and gingerly blew her nose into a pink lace hanky. Mildred couldn't tell if the sniffles were from crying or from her illness.

"What's happening?" Mildred asked, her voice sounding far away from her body.

"We're all...a bit ill," Mother replied. Her whole frame jerked, and she lifted a white hand to her mouth. "Excuse me...I'll return...shortly..."

She turned and walked hastily out of the room, clutching her abdomen.

A moment later, Marley materialized in the doorframe, clutching it with both hands as if it were a lifesaver. His dark hair was plastered to his forehead in sweaty, stringy clumps, his eyes sunken. "Mildred...are you..."

"Yes," Mildred replied brusquely.

Marley's eyes roved to the floor by the cot.

"Don't get up, honey," Aunt Camella said to Mildred. "I'll fetch some cleaning supplies and get that taken care of."

"But you're sick, too," Mildred said.

"That's no matter," Aunt Camella waved away Mildred's comment. She bustled out of the room, her footsteps a determined pitter-patter.

Mildred let her body fall back onto the cot's thin mattress, and her eyes cemented themselves shut. She had faded off into a half-unconscious delirium when a steady pattern of cool breaths by her face roused her. Expecting to rouse and see Mortem, she cringed when she came face-to-face with Marley, who was halfway on the floor with his arms hugging the cot.

"*What are you doing?*" Mildred hissed. She glanced down at the mess on the floor, which Marley knelt right in the center of, seemingly unknowingly. "Oh, dear..."

Wheezing, Marley took a moment to move a mass of hair out of his eyes. The sweat-slicked clump clung to his forehead. "I think...this is...it's not..."

"Do you really need to talk about this, whatever it is, right now?" Mildred groaned. "Go back to bed. Please."

Marley stuck out a shaking hand and grabbed Mildred's wrist. "No...this...is bad..."

"I'm aware," Mildred scoffed, pulling Marley's grip away. "It's..." A sudden, sickening thought swept over Mildred. "You don't think it's the yellow fever?" Tears smarted in her eyes and panic rose in her chest. A myriad of nightmarish images—of Morgan shrouded in black cloth, of strangers placing flowers by her own body in repose, of a gaping cavern of dirt—reeled in her head. "No, no, no...this can't be happening..."

Marley shook his head fervently. "No...it's not the fever, Millie."

"How do you know?" Mildred snapped. "You don't. You don't know everything. You don't know as much as you think you know." She angrily swiped away her tears.

"It's not," Marley insisted, his eyes wide and crazed. "I know how the fever works. This isn't...wait, hold on..." Mildred winced as he took a moment to dry heave and then collect himself. "Ugh. That was not pleasant."

"What is it, then?" Mildred asked.

Marley nodded sleepily. "Poisoning."

"*What*?" Mildred cried.

"All of us very suddenly got ill with identical symptoms," Marley breathed, rubbing his sleeve across his flushed face to mop away perspiration. "I suspect it was the cake...I knew it tasted a little strange."

"Mother and Aunt Camella did not put poison in your birthday cake!" Mildred shouted, a little too loudly. Her ears began to ring.

"Not on *purpose*," Marley said, his unblinking gaze fixed past Mildred and out the window. "Oh, look, there are pirates out on the harbor...the one with the funny hat just waved to me..."

Mildred glanced over her shoulder and, as she suspected, the view was devoid of pirates. She turned to Marley and gave him a quick slap on the head. "Stop it! You're hallucinating!"

Marley blinked a few times in rapid succession and pulled at his hair, letting out a frustrated grumble. "Damn it all...it's messing with my brain..."

While Marley contemplated his questionable mental state, Mildred pondered the legitimacy of Marley's speculation. Mother might be a thief and a liar, but she wasn't homicidal, and besides, she'd gotten sick as well. Mildred supposed

Mother could have let herself get sick to avoid any suspicion, but even that didn't seem right. Then, she remembered in a flash—for it should have been obvious from the start—Lucia's threat. Mildred gently shook Marley, who had taken to mumbling to himself.

"What did you want?" Marley lifted his head. A look of confusion suddenly crossed his face. "You know, I don't remember how I got here. And why am I kneeling in—"

"Please, this is serious," Mildred said. "Did any of your mice die?"

Marley bit his lip and glanced away.

"Marley!" Mildred barked.

"They all died," he replied.

"All of them?" Mildred was baffled.

"Yes," Marley said, his eyes cast downward.

As Marley broke into loud, dramatic weeping, Mildred explained. "Lucia doesn't want me to tell the truth about Mother. She said that unless I promised to keep it a secret, she was going to make bad things happen. The night she told me this was the night before your mice got sick. I think she was the one who put something in the cake, and if the thing she put in the cake was the same thing she poisoned the mice with..."

Mildred felt her stomach churn again, and she wasn't sure it was completely due to whatever her body was trying to purge. Marley had quit crying, but he looked pained and serious. He sighed and spoke.

"You can't listen to Lucia. She's a spoiled snob, she always was, and it seems like she always will be. You've *got* to tell the truth about Mother. It's the only way any of us are going to start to get out of this mess. Think of the bigger picture, Millie."

Mildred nodded. "You're right."

"As usual." Marley pushed himself to his feet, using the cot as balance. He dusted off his shirt and gave Mildred a nod. "Good day, sister. I bid you a restorative rest." He stumble-turned and began his journey to the door, shivering the whole time.

Mildred didn't remember falling asleep. She awoke struck by a glare of hot sunlight streaming from her window. Her head felt a little less cloudy, although a dull ache penetrated her skull. But her stomach still didn't feel quite right, and she felt uncomfortably hot and cold at the same time. She glanced down at the floor below the cot; it was shiny and clean. Aunt Camella's bed had been made up neatly. Thinking that it might do her good to get up and walk around a bit, Mildred pulled back the covers and stepped out of the cot.

She walked to her armoire and opened the double doors, intent on searching for something old and worn to wear for the remainder of the day. However, when reaching for a prospective piece of clothing, she was met with an angry face that poked through a plum-colored frock.

"Ah!" Mildred staggered backward. Lucia hurtled from inside the closet and toward Mildred, shoving her to the floor. Taken aback entirely, Mildred remained collapsed on the hardwood for a few moments, trying to shake the haze of sleep and sickness from her system enough to address the situation properly. She got to her feet and stepped towards Lucia.

"How *could* you?" Mildred scolded Lucia. "You cannot make my whole family ill because you didn't get your way. You could have *killed* someone." Mildred deliberated then gasped. "You tried to kill us!"

Lucia shook her head. "No. But I knew it was a possibility."

Mildred took a moment to compose herself, though panic had risen in her chest. "I'm sorry about what happened to you. But hurting other people doesn't change your reality."

Lucia blinked blankly. "I heard your conversation, all of it. I heard what you and Marley said about me."

"What I am going to do is the best thing for all of us," Mildred reasoned. "You don't see it now because you feel slighted and you're not being reasonable."

Lucia shook her head and glanced aside. "Go ahead with your plan, Mildred. I'm powerless now. This is what you've done to me. I'm just another forgotten-about dead girl."

Mildred couldn't think of anything to say about that, and she didn't have to, because Lucia drifted past her, out of the room, and through the open door. Mildred went to the door and scanned the hallway, but Lucia had vanished.

AND SO THERE Mildred sat, days later, at the bottom of the staircase, evaluating in her head again and again what she was going to say that night after dinner. It was to be the first one since the family had recovered from the illness that had ravaged them. (Mother had attributed it to using bad eggs in the cake batter. Aunt Camella insisted it was sun poisoning. They argued about it for half a day.)

During the meal, Mildred forced down dry chicken and watery peas despite her weak appetite. Her hands shook so much that twice her utensils went clamoring to the floor.

"For goodness sake, Mildred, stop dropping things," Mother quipped. "I simply cannot stand the constant noise. The sound of the metal hitting the hardwood floor is grating beyond measure."

"It's not the only thing that's grating beyond measure," Marley mumbled.

"Why do you always have to start an argument?" Morgan countered.

Aunt Camella picked up her water glass and began to drink very enthusiastically.

"Tell me what's so grating to you, Marley," Mother insisted. "I'd really like to know."

Father stood then, surely about to return to his study. Mother and Marley threw words at each other, and Morgan chimed in. Mildred--who saw her well-thought-out plan unraveling— declared, in a voice louder than she'd intended (she had a rushing in her ears that made it more difficult for her to hear herself): "*I* need to say something!"

The quibbling quieted. Father returned to his seat.

"What is it, Mildred?" Mother asked, accusatorily.

Mildred launched right into her confession. "I know what you've been doing, Mother. So do Marley and Mildred. You've been stealing from the yellow fever victims."

Her tongue felt numb, but her chest felt lighter.

Mother shook her head. "Mildred, I don't know what put those ideas into your head—"

"It's true," Aunt Camella interrupted. She sighed and threw her napkin on the table. "Gracious, I've been keeping silent about it for so long. It was eating me alive."

"Camella!" Mother gasped. "You cannot *possibly* believe—"

"I've known it for a while," Aunt Camella admitted. "I began to suspect something was odd when I spotted Old Widow Mary meandering around at night, moaning about her damn necklace."

Marley's fork dropped, and so did Mildred's heart.

"What are you talking about?" Mother screeched.

"From the very first day I settled in your home, I became aware of an unusual number of spirits present," Aunt Camella explained. "I suppose now is as good a time as ever to tell everyone that I'm a clairvoyant."

"And what, exactly, is that?" Father rubbed his temples.

"I can see and sometimes communicate with wandering souls—what you might call 'ghosts,'" explained Aunt Camella.

"Okay, sure," Father replied, dubiously.

"You have quite a few in your house if you'd like to know," continued Aunt Camella. "I suspect it has something to do with the nature of your business. And after they'd grown used to me being here, I was approached directly by several of them, who informed me that they'd been stolen from and lied to."

"That's not all I wanted to say," Mildred interjected. "Mother's also been using the money which was donated from victim's families to be used toward yellow fever research for her own, including for the renovation of the house."

"Oh," said Aunt Camella. "Now, I did *not* know about that."

"My God," Father breathed.

Mother, trembling, wrung her hands. A sob snapped through her. She looked broken in ways Mildred had never seen. "I'm sorry. I'm so, so sorry." She spoke in increments through her weeping. "I didn't mean for it to be taken this far, I really didn't. I feel worse and worse every day."

The room filled slowly with spirits, some of which were vaguely familiar to Mildred from that morning they'd returned from the cemetery. They convened around and above the table. It didn't appear that anyone saw them this time except for Mildred—and Aunt Camella, who glanced knowingly in Mildred's direction. Marley stared down blankly at his plate, and Morgan fixed a frown at Mother.

Father pushed back his chair and marched determinedly in the direction of his study. No one objected.

"I couldn't stand such beautiful things going to *waste*," Mother cried. "It just seemed so...wrong, for all those heirlooms to go underground. It infuriated me. I had to give up so much of my fine things, and here were these nice things which were going to be put away forever."

"And what about the donation money?" Morgan prompted.

Mother wiped her nose with a lace handkerchief. "I assumed the money was going to a lost cause. Doctors have been trying to discover treatments for years, and they can't find the answers. No one can."

Lucia had materialized behind Mother's seat, anger clear in her countenance. She gripped the back of Mother's chair on either side, her figure looming over Mother's head.

Mother blew her nose and sniffled. "But I'm so tired of excuses. It was wrong. *I* was wrong. And I should have stopped as soon as I'd begun, but it was just so difficult." She tugged off her earrings, drops of jade. She unpinned the bronze brooch at her throat and untwisted the signet ring on her pinky finger. "I am truly ashamed."

"Please, Lucia," Mildred said, although she wasn't entirely certain she'd spoken the words aloud. They seemed to be coming from somewhere outside of herself. "Please listen to her. This is her best way of showing remorse."

"Very good, Mildred," Aunt Camella spoke softly, with a smile.

Mildred felt something cool brush against her leg and looked down to see Mortem, who sat gazing up at the scene with big, sad eyes. Mildred scooped him up and held him tight.

Something in Lucia's expression softened. She lifted her hold on Mother's chai and hesitantly—delicately—placed a hand on Mother's shoulder. The tensity in the room dissipated. Lucia looked down upon Mother, and then upwards. Mildred squinted in the direction of Lucia's gaze but didn't notice a thing.

Lucia nodded, slowly. "Okay," she said to something unseen, and a smile materialized upon her face. She turned her face up to the left, her eyes shining and, in a moment, faded into soft light and then elevated out of sight.

The other specters in the room disappeared, one by one, brightly gleaming orbs in their wake. The fabled will-o-the-wisp came to Mildred's mind as she watched them float above her family's heads toward the ceiling, where they vanished.

Mother lifted her face from her handkerchief. Her eyes and nose were pink, but her tears had subsided. She blinked as if waking from a dream. "How strange. I feel as if...well, never mind."

"What just *happened?*" cried Marley, gripping the edge of the table.

There was hardly a moment to consider that, because just then Father bolted into the room, so eager in his entrance that he slipped across the polished hardwood floor, stumbling over the dining room rug. Mildred was awed; she'd never seen him more energetic in his life. He brandished a fistful of papers in one hand, a triumphant smile on his face.

"What is the matter with you?" Mother reprimanded, hand over her heart. "You escape just when something important is happening, off to your study—"

"*I've done it,*" Father gasped, sliding his glasses up the bridge of his nose.

"Get to the point!" Aunt Camella snapped her fingers.

"I've spent the last six months extensively researching the yellow fever," Father explained. "The possible origins of the disease, the symptoms, the progression of it, the effects of the disease on the vital organs—and I've discovered the following: yellow fever seems to be transferred from body to body not by bad air or by personal contact, as most people suspect, but by the *bite of a mosquito.* After that, I thought to myself, well, maybe I should think up a way to prevent that transmission. So I made a tonic that will keep the little pests away. It took weeks to perfect the recipe, but I think I've got it down. I've been using it myself and haven't been bothered by one mosquito."

"Have you been outside in all that time?" asked Morgan, reasonable as ever. (Her question was ignored.)

"You sound like a quack," Marley grumbled. "But I can't say I'm not impressed."

"*This* is what you've been doing in that silly little room of yours?" Mother screeched. "You might've told someone!"

From his vest pocket, Father procured a small glass medicine bottle filled with a clear liquid. "All one has to do is take a little bit of this mixture—" He paused to open the bottle, and poured a few drops onto a fingertip, "and apply it anywhere on the body where the skin is exposed." He dabbed the liquid behind his ear. "The ingredients in the tonic will protect anyone from mosquitoes or other pesky insects that might spread disease. And—it's completely odorless."

There was a moment of silence, and then Aunt Camella clapped her hands together excitedly. "Marvelous! Simply marvelous!"

"I plan on making a whole batch, bottling them, and selling them to the public," Father said. "The first lot should be ready by the end of this week."

"I can't believe I didn't think of this," Marley said, dumbfounded, shaking his head. "It's such an obvious conclusion."

"No, it isn't," Morgan countered.

"This may be a breakthrough," Mother said, her face lighting up. She pushed herself up from her seat. "If this is successful, we will no longer have to carry on with the funeral business."

"It will also be a major scientific advancement that will change the lives of millions," Marley added.

"Most importantly, though, it's lucrative," said Mother.

Mildred found it difficult to be joyful over the news. She'd grown to enjoy the business they'd already built and dreaded to imagine it so short-lived. She'd felt useful for the first time, helping her neighbors in need. She didn't want to give it all up now when it seemed that there was so much yet to do.

She smiled, despite her strange disappointment, as the discussion veered toward the new.

CHAPTER FIFTEEN

BY THE NEXT afternoon, the entire household was mixing tonic, carefully bottling precise amounts of the stuff. Armed with a slew of Morgan's fountain pens and inks, Morgan and Mother (whom they all agreed possessed the finest handwriting in the family) wrote out labels on Father's stationary paper, which Mildred and Marley pasted onto the bottles. At the end of the week, they'd packed a dozen crates full of the concoction, which had been christened "Mortale's Magic Mixture."

On Tuesday morning, Father put on his hat, bid everyone goodbye, and left the house with two crates of the mixture, heading out to the River Street market. He returned late in the afternoon, dejected, fatigued, and still in possession of two full crates.

"Well, it was only the first time," he noted. "People just aren't used to the idea yet."

But the following day's results weren't better, and more disappointed days drew on. Father went out in the morning, hopeful, and then trudged home downcast. No one knew what to say to him, so they all went about acting like nothing was out of the ordinary and carried on with the funeral business like normal. Although Mildred felt obligated to share in Father's disappointments, she was happier than she'd been all summer. It was a relief to be freed from the gloomy anticipation of vengeful spirits getting in the way. Everything seemed so normal, in fact, that Mildred had all but forgotten her newfound clairvoyance, and Aunt Camella's, too; ever since the fateful dinner confrontation, their revelations had been swept under the dining room rug.

After a week of Father's attempting to purvey his idea to the public unsuccessfully, he announced that he was giving it up. He settled into a chair in the drawing room and tossed his hat on the floor beside the crates of tonic bottles. Aunt Camella sat on the nearby sofa beside Mildred and Marley, all of them silently surveying him. Morgan was curled in the armchair with a book of poetry, which she'd shut upon a finger to get a good glimpse of the quiet consternation.

Mother walked in, bearing a tray of pimento sandwiches left over from the luncheons. She set it on the coffee table and frowned down upon Father.

"Why don't you take a day off tomorrow and then try once more?" Mother suggested, bringing a bit of sandwich toward his mouth. "Eat something. You look as if you're starved."

Father grumbled, weakly pushing aside the offering. Cheese glopped to the rug. Mortem jumped off Mildred's lap and ran to the drippings, head tilted as he stared longingly at the mess.

After that, everyone returned to their silent idling. Father folded his arms, staring blankly ahead and no doubt stewing over his many failures and misfortunes. Mother flipped absentmindedly through a Sears, Roebuck & Co. catalogue, periodically commenting on a cabinet or a shirtwaist that was featured. Aunt Camella drank her afternoon coffee, slurping the drink and swallowing with vigor, both of which were only amplified by the hard silence, and which made Mildred shudder. Marley gazed upon his open notebook draped across his lap, hitting his pencil against the blank paper with the enthusiasm of a marching band drummer. Morgan was absorbed in her Whitman, still as a statue except for the occasional turning of a page or pencil marking in the margins. Mildred glumly observed everyone, having the urge to speak, but then deciding that it wasn't worth the effort.

After a while, Mother got up, placed her catalogue on the table, and left the room. Aunt Camella finished her coffee and exited with her empty cup, Marley ran to the basement with his notebook, and Morgan delicately closed her book and meandered away. Mildred turned to Father. It didn't seem like he had moved a smidge the whole time.

She walked to him.

"Father," she said, softly. He didn't acknowledge her. She raised her voice. "*Father.*"

"Huh?" he snapped out of his comatose-like daydream and looked up at Mildred. "Oh, Mildred. What is the matter?"

"You *cannot* quit," Mildred said sternly. "You've put far too much time into this to stop trying after one week. And I think you already know that."

Father sighed and looked away. "Mildred, I appreciate your optimism, but you're young, and you don't see that sometimes it doesn't matter how hard you try, some things just don't work out."

Mildred's face suddenly felt flush, and she felt the heat of anger rise in her chest. "I don't think that's fair to say. I've been through a lot in a very short amount of time. I know well that sometimes things don't go as planned. But it doesn't seem like you've given this enough time to say confidently that it's not going to amount to *anything.*"

Father didn't reply for a while, but Mildred didn't go anywhere. She studied the room, listening to the tick-tock of the grandfather clock and counting the roses in the pattern of the rug. Finally, he looked up at Mildred, and something of a smile wavered on his face. He got to his feet.

"You know, you're right," he said, decidedly. "I shouldn't have to give up. And you know something else, Mildred? You are a clever young woman. Don't ever let Morgan or Marley make you think otherwise."

Mildred grinned as Father ruffled the hair on the top of her head like she was his six-year-old son instead of his thirteen-year-old daughter. But she didn't mind.

FATHER DIDN'T RETURN home the time he usually did, and Aunt Camella and Mother were anxious about his absence. Everybody was in the drawing room again: Mother with her catalogues, Marley with his notebook, Morgan with her poetry, Aunt Camella with her coffee, and Mildred with her thoughts. Mother, who had been sighing dramatically once a minute for nearly thirty minutes, exhaled the biggest sigh of them all. She looked as if she were about to voice her worry, but then the front door opened. Like cats waking from naps, everyone perked up at the sound.

Instead of Father's well-known dejected trod as he walked in and took off his jacket and hat, there were three distinctive footsteps and voices mingling in the foyer. Mother stood, slowly, and took a few steps in the direction of the door.

"What in the world is happening?" she called.

Father entered the drawing room, two unfamiliar men at either side of him, both of whom were sharply dressed. Mother rushed back into the room and resumed her seat. Mildred corrected her slouch. Marley stopped sketching but stared on with suspicion. Morgan closed her book and looked over with half-interest.

Father beamed. "You'll never believe it!"

"Believe what?" Mother asked, her attention racing from one of Father's guests to the other.

Father gestured to the man at his left. He was a bit taller than Father and wore a plaid vest, a brown bowler hat, and a neatly oiled mustache that curled at the ends. He cleared his throat. "Allow me to introduce myself. I am Professor Moribund and this—" He nodded to the shorter man who stood beside him, "is Dr. Swift. We are medical researchers visiting from Philadelphia."

"Oh, Philadelphia," Aunt Camella mused, setting down her coffee cup.

"We've been here for several months, studying yellow fever," Dr. Swift spoke. "I'm aware that this family has kept a mortuary business for about as long, and most of the victims had perished of the disease. I read a wonderful piece about it..." He took retrieved a newspaper from inside his jacket and unfolded it. "'A Fine Way to Do Dying.' By a fellow named Moxley Moorman. He did an exceptional job portraying the services you've provided to fever victims. It piqued our interest."

Mildred, who could barely contain her excitement, shot Morgan a smile. She too was smiling, her head bent to the side to conceal it.

"As it turns out, we didn't have to search very far to find one of the famed Mortales," Swift said. "We met Mr. Mortale here down by the river, where we had the honor of being introduced to this fine tonic." Moribund produced a vial from his pocket. "After listening to what prompted the creation of this mixture, and the potential of its effectiveness, Swift and I, very intrigued, proposed an agreement."

Worry strained Mother's face. "What does that mean?" Her widened eyes scrolled from Father to Moribund to Swift.

"No need for alarm, ma'am." Swift procured a stack of documents from a folder he carried under his arm. "What we are interested in is, very simply, a business transaction. We would like to purchase the tonic and bring it back to Philadelphia to be developed into a preventative treatment for the fever, and possibly other related diseases. In our hands, this could become a medical marvel. Additionally, your husband would receive a patent for his invention, and royalties for every bit of tonic bought—assuming its success. Of course, negotiations would have to take place."

Moribund lifted a hand. "That is, given you are interested in making this arrangement. We respect any decision to decline the offer."

Mother's reaction was difficult to decipher—one could have interpreted it as shock, amusement, confusion, or exasperation. She nodded, slowly at first, but then more quickly. Mildred, Marley, and Morgan exchanged glances in silence. Aunt Camella had somehow produced a fan, which she was now flapping rapidly at her flushed face. Father shook his head confusedly at Mother, brows furrowed. Before he could ask any questions, Mother jumped up and threw her arms around him.

"This is the most marvelous news we could have asked for!" Mother exclaimed. "We accept the offer."

Aunt Camella applauded enthusiastically. "Oh, wonderful! Of course, Maria, I would have supported you had you decided to decline, but really, I think this was clearly the better decision."

The rest of the evening was spent discussing various possible outcomes of the proceeding few months, mostly over dinner, which Mother had graciously invited the Professor and Doctor to join. Aunt Camella sat directly across from Doctor Swift, and Mildred, because she had been sitting next to her aunt, was acutely aware of the fact that the two were acting *very* friendly with each other.

"Ohio isn't so far away from Pennsylvania, you know," Aunt Camella mentioned, raising her wineglass to her lips with one hand and waving her fan towards her curls with the other. "Just one train ride away."

Swift smiled amusedly. "Yes, I am aware. Why do you mention it?"

"I live there," Aunt Camella replied. "I'm only a visitor here, you know. But I head home by train very soon."

"I am very glad to hear it. I return home soon as well." Swift raised his glass.

And, indeed, Aunt Camella's travel home was very near on the horizon. It seemed that most everyone had forgotten about the temporary nature of her stay. Mildred had even gotten so used to her cot that it was almost comfortable.

A week before Aunt Camella was scheduled to leave, she declared that she had an important announcement to make.

The family gathered expectantly in the parlor. Aunt Camella smiled at them all and opened her mouth to begin speaking, but instead let out a sad wail and burst into a tirade of tears. Mother ran to her with a handkerchief while Aunt Camella sniffled and bawled. After about a minute of awkwardly waiting for her hysterics to settle, a minute in which Marley rolled his eyes too many times to count and Mother grimaced, probably thinking of the state of her handkerchief into which Aunt Camella had liberally blown her nose and wiped her face, Aunt Camella took a series of calming breaths and started to speak.

"I've had the finest stay here," she began. "And as much as it pains me to have to leave, I must return home, because that's where I belong. Besides, my cat has no doubt been pining for me."

Mildred took a moment to smile down upon Mortem, who was resting peacefully in her lap. It made her wonder if Aunt Camella's cat was a live one or not.

"So," Aunt Camella sighed. "I know this is quite a big suggestion, but I would like to take Mildred back to Ohio with me."

Mildred's heart thumped in surprise.

"Whatever for?" Mother inquired.

"With her talents and work ethic, she would make a very nice assistant," Aunt Camella said. "I should clarify. I run a small business in which I aid families of victims who have been recently affected by tragedy. I help them through the grieving process. And sometimes offer other...insights, whenever they come to me, of course."

"Oh my," Mother gasped. "That's a bit much for Mildred, don't you think, Camella?"

Aunt Camella shook her head. "It's a job for natural empaths like Mildred and myself. Mildred would excel. The high school is right down the street from my house, and I have plenty of room in my home to spare."

"Well, I see no problem with it," Father said. Mother seemed surprised by his statement. "It seems very reasonable. It's a great opportunity for Mildred. Of course, it depends entirely on what Mildred thinks."

Every eye in the room roved to Mildred, who shifted uncomfortably in the heart of sudden attention. She was flattered, of course, by the suggestion that Aunt Camella thought she was good enough to be an assistant to her in her work. But she had never left home before, and though she had gotten to be more familiar with her aunt throughout her stay, they were still not close confidantes. She tucked a bit of hair behind her ear and spoke directly to Aunt Camella.

"I'm thankful," Mildred said. "But I don't think I can accept."

Aunt Camella's eyes dimmed with disappointment, but she nodded. She looked as if she were about to cry again, so Mildred jumped into an explanation.

"It's not that I don't think it would be a good thing," she tried to explain. "But I don't think I would be able to go without Morgan or Marley. You see, I've never left home before, and I would hate to have to do it alone. You think I'm the kind of person you're looking for, but Morgan and Marley are two of the most magnificent people you'll ever come across."

Marley nodded enthusiastically.

"Mildred, I don't think it's appropriate for you to turn Aunt Camella's kind offer into some sort of compromise," Mother scoffed.

"I don't take offense at all to the suggestion," Aunt Camella said. "In fact, I think it's quite good. I never considered it. Why take one when I can take three?"

"But...all three of them," Mother stuttered. "Who will help with the services? And how long would they be gone? Having all three of them leave, just like that..."

"There's the telephone," Marley reminded her.

Mother's instant glare evoked the memory of the incident that resulted in their telephone being ripped from the wall and which had yet to be replaced.

"Uh, you could get a new one, I mean."

"Here's what we'll do," Father spoke. "We'll give it a month or two and see how this patent and deal with the tonic turns out. If everything goes as it's meant to, we'll be able to hire help again—and we'll buy a new telephone."

"But I leave next week." Aunt Camella looked sad all over again.

"Can you extend your stay?"

Aunt Camella looked off to the side and shook her head. "I'd like to get home as soon as I can...but I will be expecting to hear from you, should things go as planned or not. If they do, by God, send at least one of them to me."

Mildred thought about how she wouldn't have to spend many more nights sleeping atop a rickety old cot or having to share her room. She thought about the funeral business coming to an end, along with the fever. She looked around the room. Bright white-yellow sunlight flooded through the window. Mother and Father sat side-by-side. Morgan and Marley sat on either side of her, leaning over her to talk to one another, but she didn't mind. Aunt Camella smiled warmly in Mildred's direction.

Mildred ran a hand along Mortem's cool fur, feeling that, for the first time in a long time, things just might be getting better.

CHAPTER SIXTEEN

ON THE LAST day in September, it rained. Mildred listened to it drumming against the house as she sat on the bottom stair, her travel case at her feet and an expectant hope at the brim of her heart. The front door opened, and Mother stepped inside, closing her big black umbrella.

"Mildred, go get your brother and sister," she said. "The carriage is here."

Minutes later, the three of them were securing their things atop the carriage, the driver balancing a measly umbrella above them and failing miserably to keep any of them dry, including himself. Once everything was situated, the driver nodded and said he'd wait for them to say their goodbyes as he made his way back around to the driver's seat.

After a water-addled few minutes of goodbyes—from the rain and a generous number of tears—Mother and Father gave each one a final hug and retreated from the rain.

Decisively, Marley nodded.

"Well, if that's it, I'm going in, thank you very much," he said. He saluted Mildred and Morgan and slipped inside the waiting carriage, shutting the door from the shower. Mildred looked at Morgan, who was shivering, and they smiled at each other, thinking of how foolish they must have looked.

"We really should be going," Morgan said. "The train arrives at the station in less than an hour."

Mildred nodded in agreement, but then a thought came to her. She turned and took off for the house. Morgan called after her. "*What are you doing?*"

Hopping up the front porch steps, throwing open the front door, and sliding into the foyer, Mildred searched the space anxiously, ignoring the fact that she was dripping onto Mother's precious polished floors. "Mortem! Mortem, where are you?"

She rushed into the drawing room, eagerly eyeing the sofa, the armchair, and the coffee table. She knelt on the rug and peeked between the legs of the furniture.

She heard the soft sound of padding feet and scrambled to stand. From the hall, Mortem walked into view and sat beside the wall underneath the drawing room doorway.

"Come here," Mildred pleaded.

Mortem blinked. Mildred glanced out the window; inside the carriage, Marley and Morgan awaited her anxiously.

"Mortem," Mildred said once more.

The cat didn't budge.

Mildred approached him and bent to his level. He looked up with a tilted head. She ran a hand down his back.

"I'm leaving," she said. "And I won't be back for a long while."

He sniffed her fingers.

"A part of me thought you'd come with me," Mildred said.

Mortem turned and trotted away.

"Hey!" Mildred called, following him into the foyer.

He hopped up onto the first step of the staircase and settled in the corner. Mildred knew that this is where he was going to stay.

She left the house for the final time and shut the door. What had been torrents minutes before had slowed to a faint drizzle. Mildred walked to the carriage, stumbling over the slick cobblestone. Once inside, Morgan nudged Mildred and motioned to the sky through the open window of the vehicle.

Mildred turned her attention upwards as the carriage pulled away from the house. Although the rain continued to fall, and the clouds still were fierce and grey, the sky was a pleasant blue, and the sun was bright and hot against her skin.

"It's beautiful, and sad, at the same time, isn't it?" said Morgan.

And so it was.

HISTORICAL NOTE
ON YELLOW FEVER

Memento Mortale is a work of fiction, and as such small liberties were taken to serve the story.

There wasn't anyone who concocted a miracle repellent that would keep disease-carrying insects at bay. The actual path to discovering the cause of yellow fever outbreaks was a bit more complicated.

After the American Civil War, they weren't any major yellow fever outbreaks in the United States. However, yellow fever epidemics did greatly affect many places at various times in history. Perhaps the most famous epidemic of yellow fever in the United States occurred in Philadelphia, Pennsylvania in 1793. It is estimated that ten percent of the total city's population perished from the disease.

Yellow fever is a disease that is spread through the bite of an infected mosquito, which meant that breakouts of the fever were more likely to happen in port cities—like Savannah—and places near large bodies of water, where mosquitoes linger.

Modern medicine was in its infancy at the time of these epidemics, so not knowing how the sickness started or how it spread struck fear in many people. The belief that foul air spreads illness (known as *miasma*) was popular at the time, as well as the belief that epidemics were the result of divine or cosmic punishment.

The discoverer that mosquitoes were the carriers and transmitters of the disease was James Carroll, a physician for the United States Army, and his partner, Walter Reed, in 1900.

Today, a case of yellow fever is extremely rare in the United States and other developed countries and can be treated quite effectively with modern medicine. Unfortunately, many third-world countries still suffer yellow fever casualties due to their lack of proper medical resources.

ABOUT THE AUTHOR

Angeline Walsh is a filmmaker and amateur historian from Cleveland, Ohio. As a child, she once followed a man dressed in Gothic Victorian wardrobe into Disney's Haunted Mansion. Her work has been described as "not marketable," "weird," and "too dark for children." She blames her morbidity on having visited one too many catacombs as a child.

Her poetry collection, *Bad Psychiatry and Other Aptly Titled Poems* was released in 2018 to critical acclaim.* Her historical dark comedy series, *The Coroner's Assistant,* is currently streaming on Tubi.* *

*This is a lie.

* *Funnily enough, *The Coroner's Assistant* has received critical acclaim.